rother Louis,
mpanion.

Blemished Heart

To my dear friend Pattie,
I hope my story
will be a blessing
to you.
Love,
Fern Boldt
12/4/2014

4

Fern Boldt

...51

...ces
...45

Contents

Preface

In January of 2014, I started an online novel writing course. I had only written short picture books and could never figure out how people could write a story with tens of thousands of words.

My instructor, Sarah Aronson, suggested I make a map of the area where I grew up and then write down everything I could remember. This was to evoke memories for scenes that my characters could act out. I always feared writing a story based on my childhood. Some of it is extremely painful and embarrassing to talk about. Sarah said, "Fern, just write." The thought that someone might benefit from my story became my encouragement to continue.

It only took five months to write the whole story, then another couple of months to edit. It has been quite a journey.

The main character is Lizzy Bauman. Also included are her parents, two older brothers, Clyde and Jimmy, and a younger sister Molly.

The author, Fern Boldt, at the age of eight.

Lizzy unwillingly accumulates dark spots on her heart every time she gets into trouble or suffers a painful event. She records her misdeeds in a little book and desperately tries to rid her soul of them, and avoid getting more, without much luck.

Lizzy becomes desperate and wants to escape her abusive home, but has no place to go. Poverty, a strict father, an abusive brother and an unresponsive mother keep her hostage until the day God provides a way for her to leave.

Parts of the story are difficult to read, but keep going. It will get better. Buckle up! You're in for a wild ride.

Acknowledgments

I owe a deep debt of gratitude to the many people who helped me write this book. Sarah Aronson, through writers.com, taught me the basics of writing a novel. She encouraged me to keep going when I nearly gave up after the first few weeks, because I found it too painful to write.

Fellow writer, Dianne Matich talked me into taking the novel writing course, and then walked with me every step of the way to its completion. She encouraged me to expand each scene: "Don't just *tell* me you had health inspections in your rural school. *Show* me what they were like."

I extend my gratitude to Dianne Matich, Jennifer Mook-Sang, Jodi Cardillo and Wendy Whittingham from my local critique group for cheering me on month after month and for helping me to improve the story. I also received help from an online critique group, including Anny, Ashley, Emily, Jeri, Kathy, Robin, Sandra and Tina. Their suggestions were extremely helpful.

Several of my friends and relatives read early copies of my novel and encouraged me to publish it. You kept me going.

A special "thank you" goes to my son Ted Boldt for suggesting the title, *Blemished Heart*. It fits the story perfectly.

I appreciate my editor, Sara Davison, for polishing my story. It has been a pleasure to work with her.

Thank you to the staff at Word Alive Press, especially to those who designed the cover and created this beautiful book.

How can I ever thank David Bowman, the artist who made the illustration of Jesus and the little girl, which can be found in chapter twenty-six? It touches my heart deeply every time I see it.

Above all, thank you to my husband Peter, who put up with the long hours it took to write my story. He's one in a million.

I

Disastrous Morning

THE WALLS OF OUR RICKETY, DRAFTY, TWO-STORY FARMHOUSE COULDN'T resist the howling winds. Our family lived near Howells, Nebraska in the early 1950s, where my father worked as a farm laborer. He and my mother looked after my siblings and me—older brothers Clyde and Jimmy, and our little sister Molly. The cramped and cluttered downstairs had a living room, a kitchen and my parents' bedroom. A narrow, creaky stairway led upstairs to where the boys slept in one bedroom and the girls in the other.

The enclosed back porch held a pile of split logs, a bushel basket of corncobs for the kitchen stove and a place for the family dog Buster to lie down. Along one wall, Dad had pounded in a few nails to hang our coats. A strip of farm machinery belt, eighteen inches long, two inches wide and a quarter of an inch thick, hung on one of these—the strap.

≈

I slept above the living room. Every morning of my eight years, I woke to the crash of my dad firing up the potbellied stove before going out to milk the cows. Shaking the grate to loosen the ashes from the preceding day's fire made enough racket to wake the dead. He wrapped a few corncobs with newspaper, doused them with a bit of kerosene and lit them with a match. I listened for the "woof" sound as they burst into flames. He added some chopped wood to the fire and bundled up to go out to the barn.

Before he left, he hollered up the stairs, "Clyde, git yourself down here. It's time to go milkin'."

"It's too dang cold to milk them blasted cows," Clyde grumbled. But he soon dressed and went downstairs. No one disobeyed when Dad called.

I checked the thermometer I had sneaked into my bedroom. It had shown 12°C/54°F at bedtime, but this morning it had fallen to 1°C/34°F.

I glanced out the window to see if it had stopped snowing, but I couldn't see a thing. A thick layer of ice covered the glass. I scratched my name, Lizzy, into the frost. I didn't have to be up for another two hours, so I tucked myself back under the covers and fell asleep while the house warmed.

I woke to Mom calling, "Jimmy, Lizzy, it's time to git up for school. Breakfast is almost ready."

I hesitated before leaving the warm pile of blankets. I grabbed a fresh set of clothes from the dresser, flew downstairs and started to dress behind the potbellied stove in the living room. I didn't own a pair of pajamas, so I slept in the dress I had worn the day before.

Cob shed, outhouse, chickens, kitten and dog on the farm where the author grew up

"Git out of here! I'm dressin'," I shouted. My brothers would have to stay in the kitchen for a couple of minutes until I finished. Then they would take their turns.

As soon as I dressed, Mom put me to work. "Keep this stove stoked with cobs, so the fire don't go out. I have to help Dad run the milk through the separatin' machine before breakfast."

I crossed my legs. "But I have to pee, and it snowed last night."

"Well, you can use the night pot. But hurry, 'cause I need help," Mom said.

We didn't have an indoor bathroom, only an outhouse. It had three sizes of holes in the seat board, large, medium and small—for the different-sized family members. I always chose the small one so I wouldn't fall through. That would be a disaster.

We couldn't afford to buy toilet paper so we used old newspapers or the dull pages out of the Sears and Roebuck or 'Monkey' Ward catalogues. The shiny ones with pictures didn't work well. If I crumpled the page and rubbed it together for a few seconds, it became softer. If we had no catalogues or newspapers, we could always use a corncob. We had a whole shed full of those.

Tromping out in the cold through a foot of snow—especially when I needed to hurry—presented a challenge. However, we did have a solution for that: a small pail with a lid on it, that we kept in the back porch, where we had no privacy. We were supposed to use it for going "number one." Woe to the person who happened to leave the lid off, especially if some "idiot" hadn't obeyed the previous rule.

I quickly peed and started stoking the fire. I tried to be careful not to burn myself, but that morning I touched the scorching hot lid and hollered, "Ow! That's hot!"

Mom took a quick look at my hand. "Be more careful there. We ain't got no money to take you to a doctor."

Between stokes of the fire, I pumped water from a little hand pump by the kitchen sink and poured it into the reservoir on the end of the kitchen stove. The health department had deemed the water unsafe to drink from the cistern, but we could use it for baths and laundry. Otherwise, we had to bring in all our water from a well out by the barn.

When Dad and Clyde came in from the barn, they ran the milk through the separator and put things away. Then they came to the kitchen table. Clyde, Jimmy and I sat on a bench on one side of the table against the wall. Dad and Mom sat on the other side, with my sister Molly between them in her high chair.

Dad read a few verses from the Bible and prayed the same prayer every morning, even yawning on the same sentence each time. Then Clyde, Jimmy and I took turns saying, "Come, Lord Jesus, be our guest. Let these gifts to us be blessed." Then we could dig in.

We usually ate oatmeal for breakfast, as it cost little to make for a family of six. We always had lots of milk to drink. It didn't take long to scarf it all down. Soon we would have to leave for school.

Whoever nailed the bench together put the leg boards too far in from the end, which made it tip easily. Clyde waited until Jimmy left the table, then he quickly jumped up off his end and sent me flying. He gave me an evil smirk.

Mom saw me sitting on the floor. "You're so clumsy, Girl. Hurry up and put your coat on. It's time to walk to school."

"Walk? Ain't you goin' to drive us? It's cold today."

"No, Dad has to feed the cattle. Molly had another seizure last night, so I can't take you neither."

"Oh, poop."

"Clyde and Jimmy will walk with you. It ain't but two miles." She lifted Molly out of her highchair.

"Can I wear my snow pants?"

"Yeah, but make sure you take them off when you git there. You know Dad won't let you wear them at school."

"Yes, Mommy."

I put on my coat, but couldn't find my mittens or hat. "Where's my stuff?" I hollered. "I put them in my coat sleeve yesterday, so I could find them this mornin'. I'm gonna freeze on the way to school."

Clyde tossed them at me. "Hurry up, Dummy. We're gonna be late."

"Where'd you hide my things?"

"None of your business." He smacked me on the back.

By the time I finished putting my boots on, I felt frazzled, and my burned hand hurt. I didn't relish the idea of walking to school on such a dreadfully cold, snowy day. I wondered if I would be able to keep up with my brothers, and what Clyde would do to me, if I didn't. I had no choice, so I grabbed the one-gallon Karo syrup bucket that contained my homemade bread and jelly sandwich, and faced the long trek to District 11.

A Cold Walk
to School

THE WIND HOWLED. SNOW BLEW IN MY FACE AND NEARLY FROZE MY NOSE off. I hoped I would survive the trek to school. We had to walk a half-mile west and one and a half miles south on a gravel country road, which now had a foot of snow covering it. We walked single file in the tracks the cars had made. Clyde tromped along first on his long legs. Jimmy followed and I scrambled to keep up behind him.

A bull snorted at us as we walked past the neighbor's fence. His breath made two large puffs of steam in the frosty air. We turned the corner to go south and started to climb up the first hill. A dog raced out of the driveway with bared teeth, threatening to shred our legs.

"Shut up!" Clyde whumped him on the head with his lunch pail. Thwok! The dog went whimpering back to the house.

At the top of the second hill we passed our church, Bethlehem Chapel, on the left. Down that hill on the right lived the Brandon boys, who enjoyed teasing the life out of me at school. We had to trudge up one last hill, where District 11, our one-room school, stood at the crest.

Clyde, five years older than I, kept yelling the whole way, "Hurry up, or we'll be late for school!"

"I'm hurryin' as fast as I can," I said.

"Wait up, Clyde! Lizzy can't go that fast," Jimmy said.

"She should 'a thought about that before she took so long to git dressed," he said. "She'd better move it, or I'll learn her to git goin'."

At least I'll be able to pass health inspection this morning. I cleaned up real good.

I don't know how we made it there in one piece. We made a mad dash up the steps to the front porch of our one-room school, arriving as Miss Richter rang the warning bell that classes would start in five minutes.

We hung up our coats in the coatroom and yanked off the boots we had pulled on over our shoes. I still shivered from the long walk so I kept my snow pants on. The boys wore overalls and didn't have to worry about bare legs like I did.

I hope my brothers don't notice I still have my snow pants on.

Our small school contained one large classroom, a small library and a coatroom. We put our lunch buckets on a shelf at the back of the room. Near the entryway stood a water bucket with an enameled dipper, from which we all drank.

The classroom had four rows of desks, with four or five seats in each row. They had been bolted on to wooden runners so the teacher could move several of them at once when she cleaned. I ran to mine and plunked down.

We started the day by standing beside our desk and saluting the flag. I placed my burned right hand over my pounding heart. "I pledge allegiance to the flag of the United States of America and to the Republic for which it stands, one nation under God, indivisible, with liberty and justice for all." In warm weather, we stood around the flagpole outside for this exercise, but not today.

Then Miss Richter called the roll for the second grade class.

"Nancy Vlasta."

"Present."

"Kathy Petracek."

"Present."

"Elizabeth Bauman."

"Present," I squeaked.

"Elizabeth, speak up. I can barely hear you," she said. "Besides, you're so skinny, if you sit sideways in your desk, I can't see you. I almost counted you absent."

The Brandon brothers snickered. Clyde guffawed.

I dropped my head and slid further down in my seat as a flush crept across my cheeks.

After all sixteen of us had answered roll call, the humiliating health inspections began. Either the teacher, or one of the older students, stopped by each desk and asked us several questions. If we passed, we received a white sticker in the shape of an Ivory soap bar to put on the chart. If we had only one infraction, we received a yellow sticker, two things, a red sticker, and a black sticker for more than two infractions.

I watched Miss Richter check out Clyde. He always looked like a horse that had been "rode hard and put away wet."[1]

"Did you comb your hair?"

"Yup." His rooster tail shot straight up on the top of his head.

"It looks like someone ran an eggbeater through it," she said. "Did you brush your teeth?"

"I didn't have no time."

She asked him to lean his head sideways so she could check his ears.

"Those look like they haven't been washed for a week," she said. "You could plant potatoes in there."

His face turned red. Jimmy and I glanced at each other and snickered.

"Let me see your hands."

Clyde slowly pulled them out of his lap and placed them on top of his desk.

"You have dirt under your fingernails," she said. "You're going to clean them right after I finish inspection."

"Okay, Miss Richter."

She continued on with her questions. "Are you wearing clean clothes?"

"Yeah, I put them on this morning."

She pinched her nose. "They smell like a cow barn."

"I had to help Dad with the milkin'."

"Here's your black sticker. Go put it on the chart."

His head dropped, and he shuffled over to it.

She went on to the next student.

I had spent a few extra minutes cleaning myself up and passed inspection with flying colors. I gloated a bit as I marched up to put my *beautiful* Ivory soap sticker on the chart. As I walked back to my desk, Clyde scowled at me. I stuck my tongue out at him.

≈

Clyde came up to me at recess. "Why are you still wearin' them snow pants? You know what Dad said about that. Girls ain't s'posed to wear men's clothes."

"I was cold."

"I'm tellin' Dad when we git home. You're gonna git a lickin'."

I sat down and started to pull them off. "Don't tattle on me."

"I saw you, and I'm tellin'."

I finished pulling them off. "And I'm tellin' Mom you got a black sticker."

"Oh, no, you're not."

I hung the snow pants in the coatroom before classes started again. Despite my bold words, I felt terrified the rest of the day.

Why can't I wear them when I'm cold? Doesn't anyone care if I'm freezing to death? But if Dad says it's in the Bible, it must be true. He's gonna beat me again.

I dreaded the walk home worse than the one going to school that morning. I dressed quickly so I wouldn't hold Clyde up this time. When we reached the house on the last hill near our farm, Clyde decided to take a shortcut through the neighbor's pasture.

"Why do we have to walk through the pasture?" I asked.

"It saves a quarter of a mile of walking, that's why," he said.

Not only did the deep snow make it difficult to keep up with the boys, but we also had to climb through a barbed wire fence between the neighbor's farm and ours.

"I can't crawl through that by myself," I said.

"I'll hold the wires apart." Jimmy stepped closer to the fence.

Clyde knocked his arm away. "No, I will."

He stepped his boot on the bottom wire and pulled up on the top one. Jimmy slipped right through.

I hesitated. "You aren't gonna let go, are you?"

"I might. Hurry up, you idiot!"

I climbed through so quickly I fell face first into the snow. I tried to brush it off with my mittens, but they were soaked. I felt so miserable. I started to wail.

Clyde slapped me on the back. "Shut up, crybaby."

I stopped crying, but my heart felt broken.

Why is Clyde always so mean to me? I wish he had someone bigger to whop him around sometimes.

Mom took one look at me when we arrived home and said, "Why'd you kids go through the field?"

Clyde shrugged. "It's a shortcut."

Mom ignored him and glared at me, both hands on her hips. "Now your snow pants are full of cockle burrs."

"I didn't want to do it. Clyde made me."

She started picking off the burrs. I helped, but the sharp points hurt my burned hand.

Clyde came by and said, "Lizzy didn't take her snow pants off when she got to school."

"Is that true?"

"Yes, Mommy. I kept them on until I warmed up."

"Well, you know the rules. Dad's gonna hear about this when he comes in from the barn."

"Please don't tell him. I won't do it again." Then I quietly added, "Clyde got a black sticker on the health chart today." But she appeared not to have heard me.

Clyde waited until Mom was out of earshot. "You'd better keep your mouth shut, skuzz bucket. What I do in school is none of your business. Now you're gonna git it from Dad *and* me."

When I heard Dad coming in, I ran upstairs and hid under the covers. I heard Mom say, "Lizzy left her snow pants on at school today."

"It looks like that girl needs to learn a lesson about keepin' the rules around here."

I listened with dread to the sound of his heavy footsteps tromping to the back porch. I visualized him removing the strap from its nail. Then I heard his feet stomping up the narrow stairway. He raged into my room, threw the blankets aside and yanked me out of bed.

"No, Daddy. Don't hit me." I held my hands behind me to protect myself.

"Why did you wear your snow pants at school?"

"I was cold."

"That's no excuse," he said. "The teacher has a fire going in the furnace every day."

Whack! Whack! Whack!

"Ow! Ow! Ow!"

"Next time, don't break my rules," he said.

"But I was cold, Daddy." I started to sob.

"Your butt is warm now, ain't it?"

After he left, I flooded my pillow with tears.

That hurt so much. Why can't I learn to obey all his rules? Why am I such a bad girl?

I felt a dark spot smudge my heart that day. I determined to be a more obedient daughter. Even if Dad's rules didn't make sense, I would try to keep them. I cried myself to sleep.

III

Early School Years

KINDERGARTEN SOUNDED EXCITING TO ME. I COULD BARELY WAIT until August of 1949, when I turned five. We lived in Columbus then. Clyde, Jimmy and I attended District 3, about a mile and a half from home. Dad, Mom, or one of the other kids' parents, drove us every day, since we lived beside the railroad. Crossing the tracks twice daily would have been unsafe for us kids, aged ten, seven, and five.

I loved to play with modeling clay and made all sorts of strange critters. Once, I rolled a gray piece into a long snake. I made a big fat head, poked little eyes into it with my pencil, and added a forked tongue. I tucked 'Slithers' into my desk and pondered what I would do with this scary creature.

When the bell rang for recess, I pulled it quietly out of my desk and placed it in the pocket of my dress. Once outside, I whipped it out and started to chase one of the first grade boys.

"There's a poisonous snake after you," I hissed. "S-s-s-s-s!"

He took off running, and I chased him. When he came around the front of the school, he ran in and told the teacher what I had done. She called me in and pulled me aside.

"Elizabeth, Chucky said you chased him with a snake," she said.

"It's just clay." I frowned. "It ain't that scary."

"It scared Chucky, though, and he has a bad heart," she said. "His doctor says he's not supposed to run. He could die if he gets too worked up. You must *never* do that again."

"I'm sorry," I said. "I didn't know. I won't do that no more."

She confiscated my charming snake, squashed it into a ball and put it away in the cupboard.

My poor little 'Slithers' had such a short life, but I feel bad that I nearly killed Chucky. I'm a naughty girl again today.

≈

One of the other mothers, Mrs. Galina, took turns with my parents picking us up from school. She was usually in a hurry, but one day she decided to have a chat with the teacher, which took a lot longer than I expected.

I had to pee or I soon would wet my pants. I did the "rain dance" and crossed my legs, but it didn't help. Mrs. Galina kept talking. Finally, I couldn't wait a second longer and raced to the outhouse. I didn't have time to tell anyone.

In warm weather, the smell in the outhouse could knock you over. Fat, creepy-looking spiders stared down at me from their tangled webs. They gorged themselves on unsuspecting flies up in the corners. They always frightened me, and I usually asked someone to go with me. This time I couldn't wait. I hopped up on the smallest hole, barely making it in time.

When I finished, I ran as fast as I could, but it wasn't fast enough for Mrs. Galina. She had started driving away without me.

I waved my arms and yelled, "Wait for me!"

She stopped the car and backed into the schoolyard again.

When I hopped into the car, she screamed at me. "When I'm ready to go, you'd better be in the car. Next time I'll leave you here."

"Okay, Mrs. Galina." Tears trickled down my cheeks. Jimmy put his arm around my shoulders.

Why am I always getting into trouble? Will I ever learn to be good? I suppose that's another dark spot on my heart.

≈

In the middle of my Kindergarten year, the son of my dad's boss decided he wanted to live in the house we occupied and we had to move. Dad found a different farmhand job near Howells and moved our family there.

That's where I met Miss Richter, who was tall and slim, with long straight brown hair, a beaked nose and piercing dark eyes. She yelled a lot and rigorously enforced her rules with harsh discipline. All she lacked was a black hat and a broom. I had heard a lot of yelling at home, but she intimidated me even more.

We sat in rows facing the teacher. The front of the room had a blackboard with the alphabet written neatly at the top in both printing and cursive writing. I sat in the smallest desk in the room because I was so tiny. Kathy and Nancy, the only other students my age, sat in the row beside me and we became inseparable friends.

When the teacher wanted our class to come up to her desk for a lesson, she called for us and we went and sat on little square chairs made out of old orange crates. After she finished teaching us, we returned to our desks to do our homework while the next class had its lesson. I learned a lot by listening to her teach the older children.

One day in Kindergarten, while the teacher instructed one of the other classes, Kathy leaned over to me and whispered. "What did she ask us to draw?"

"Our farm," I whispered back.

"No, our family," Nancy said, a bit too loud.

Miss Richter turned around and yelled, "Okay, you three girls. I'm keeping you after school for a detention."

My heart started pounding. I imagined what horrible things she could do to us. I grabbed my book and pencil and started drawing like crazy.

Worse yet, I feared what my parents would do when they found out I had caused trouble in school. Clyde would surely tell my dad, and he would whip me when he came home from work.

I tried to draw our house and barn, but I was so scared. I made wavy lines instead of straight. My coloring didn't stay inside the lines. I made a mess of it.

After the other students left at the end of the day, Miss Richter made us three girls stay at our desks and started yelling at us again.

"Why can't you keep quiet while I'm teaching the other classes? I gave you enough work to keep you busy."

"Yes, Miss Richter," Nancy said.

She began to clean the classroom. As she swept the floor, she punctuated her shouts with whacks on our heads with her straw broom.

"I saw you whispering." She whopped Nancy on the head. "What was that about?"

No one dared say a word.

"I'm waiting, Nancy. What did you say to the other girls?"

"Kathy wanted to know what you asked us to draw."

"I had told you what to draw. How could you forget that fast?" She whacked Kathy on the head with the broom.

"I didn't know if you asked for a picture of our farm or our family. Lizzy said you wanted a scene from our farm and Nancy said you wanted us to draw our family."

"Is that true, Lizzy?"

"Yes."

Whack! My heart started to throb.

"Well, I don't want any more whispering going on while I'm teaching. Do you understand that?"

"Yes, Miss Richter."

She gave us each a last whack on our heads and dismissed us.

We slinked out of school. Jimmy had waited for me, but Clyde had run on home. He wanted to make sure my parents heard *the truth* before I arrived. Our parents always supported the teacher. If she disciplined us at school, it meant double punishment at home.

I tried to creep into the house, but Mom met me at the door. "I heard you caused trouble in school today," she said. "Wait until your father comes home. He'll make sure that doesn't happen again."

I went to my room and awaited my punishment. I stuffed a doll blanket into my underwear.

Maybe I should use a pillow.

When Dad came in that evening, Mom didn't wait until after supper to tell him I had gotten into trouble at school. He came up to my room.

"When are you gonna learn to obey your teacher?"

"I'll try, Daddy."

It didn't do any good to plead my case. Dad tried and convicted me without a jury. No one heard a peep from the defendant. My sentence remained the same—a beating with the strap. The blanket in my pants didn't help a bit. My bottom stung with pain. Every time my dad whipped me unfairly, I got so angry I felt like another dark spot was added to my soul.

Later, hunger drove me downstairs for supper. Clyde grinned from ear to ear as I entered the kitchen.

When my parents were out of earshot, I stuck my tongue out at him and said, "Tattletale, tattletale, hangin' on a skunk's tail. Next time I'm tellin' on you."

He balled up his fists. "You do that, and I'll beat the crap out of you."

I backed away. Sometimes I really hated being so small.

≈

When we learned how to print the alphabet, we each had a notebook with lines in it. Miss Richter told us to make each letter stop exactly at the top line and not go below the bottom one. She expected it to look neat.

I would print each letter, erase it and reprint it until it looked almost like the one in the lesson. Sometimes, I erased it so many times, I wore the page through. Then I'd tear it out of my book and start over. The more the teacher complimented my handwriting, the harder I tried to perfect it. I made many trips to the pencil sharpener by the teacher's desk.

I'm gonna do this as perfect as possible, so she'll tell me I did a good job.

Miss Richter didn't tolerate left-handed people. I watched her teach a penmanship lesson to the older students. One of the eighth graders, Kathy's brother Joseph, wrote his lesson with his left hand.

"Joseph, use your right hand," she yelled.

"But I can write better with my left."

"I don't care. My students will all learn to write with their right hand."

Every time she saw him writing with his left hand, she walked past his desk and cracked his knuckles with a ruler. He reluctantly changed back to his right hand.

≈

Daniel, one of the younger boys, acted up whenever he thought Miss Richter wasn't watching. He made funny faces at the other kids, causing them to laugh and incur the teacher's wrath. He could never sit still for five minutes. If his lips were ever silent, he chattered with his fingertips. At recess, he ate box elder bugs off the cement school wall to make the girls feel sick.

When Miss Richter had enough of his antics, she hauled him to the library off the main classroom, yelled at him and slapped him. The rest of us cringed, as we could hear every word she said and every smack she laid on him. When he came back out, red blotches and scratches covered his face. We felt sorry for him.

His father, rumored to be mean to him at home, would surely punish him again after school. We never dared to ask. I had enough to worry about from my own father.

≈

Every six weeks, our teacher sent home a report card to let our parents know how we did in school. Mom promised to give us ten cents for every A, and five cents for every B.

17

On the day we received our reports, I ran home from school as fast as I could and found Mom in the kitchen kneading bread.

"Look, Mom!" I waved my report card in front of her face. "I have five A's and one B+."

"Well, ain't that good?" She wiped her hands on her apron. "I've saved up a few coins for you kids." She traipsed to her bedroom and fetched her purse. "Here's five dimes and a nickel."

"Thanks, Mom," I raced off to hide my new treasure in my bedroom and returned in time to see Jimmy give his report to her.

"Mom, I have an A, and five B's. That's purdy good, ain't it?"

"It sure is, Jimmy." She wiped her hands again and fetched some coins out of her apron pocket. Here's three dimes and a nickel for you."

He stuck them in his pocket and jingled them as he started to walk away.

Mom went back to peeling potatoes for supper. "Where's Clyde?"

Jimmy shrugged his shoulders. "I don't know."

"I want to see if he did better this time." She crossed the room and pushed open the screen door. "Clyde, git in here. I want to see your report card."

Clyde shuffled into the house. "I ain't showin' it to nobody."

"I have to sign it to send back to your teacher," she said. "Now give me that thing."

Clyde reluctantly handed it over.

"Five D's and an F? What's goin' on with you?"

"I hate school. The kids laugh at me when I can't answer the teacher's questions."

"You have to finish school, if you want to git a good job someday." She signed his report card.

"I'm gonna work on a farm, so I don't need to know nothin'."

"You're staying in school. You can try harder this next six weeks."

Later, Clyde saw me skipping around the house. "What's the matter with you?"

I stopped and shook my head. "Nothin'."

"I s'pose you got lots of money for your report card."

"Yup! Fifty-five cents this time." I hoped my hiding place was safe.

"You're the teacher's pet."

"No, I ain't! I do all the work she gives me. Besides, I see you staring out the window instead of studying."

"Oh, shut up, or I'll clobber you."

I stared at him. *Who made you my boss?*

IV

My Sister Molly

MY BABY SISTER MOLLY WAS BORN AT THE END OF MY KINDERGARTEN year, a few months before I turned six. Mom had lost two babies between the two of us, a boy and a girl who died soon after birth. My parents didn't allow me to attend the graveside service of either one of them, so I can't tell you what it was like. I know my parents were sad for a long, long time after each of their deaths.

You can imagine our happiness when Molly arrived. She had dark brown curls, chocolate eyes and a smile that melted our hearts. When she was only a few weeks old, I heard her crying in her crib. Mom, kneading bread in the kitchen, didn't pay any attention.

Her cries became more intense. "Mommy, Molly's crying."

"I need to finish making this bread dough. She'll be fine. When she gits finished hollerin', she'll go back to sleep."

Mom isn't listening. I can't let my little sister cry like that.

I pulled myself up onto the railing, reached into the crib and put my hands under her arms. I dragged her over to the edge of the mattress and scraped her body up over the railing. I could barely carry her, and she almost slipped out of my grasp. Mom shrieked when she saw me dangling Molly by her underarms.

"What in heaven's name are you doing? Molly can't even hold her own head up yet."

"She was cryin'. I'm tryin' to help."

"If she cries and I don't hear her, come and git me. You're too little to pick her up."

Mom scooped up my wailing sister, leaving floury handprints on her back.

"I did call you and call you, but you didn't come."

"I had to finish kneading the bread."

My heart ached for Molly. Did Mom leave *me* crying in the crib when I was a baby? I could now understand how possible that was. I decided to keep an eye on my sweet baby sister, so she wouldn't feel lonely and abandoned, like I did.

≈

One Sunday, we visited Dad's sister and her husband, Aunt Lola and Uncle Abe. They came out of the house to greet us when they saw us driving up the long driveway.

"Wie gehts?" (How are you?) Uncle Abe asked in his usual German greeting.

"The gates are fine, but the fence is crooked," Dad joked.

When my aunt and uncle noticed the cast on my mom's arm, they looked alarmed. "What on earth happened?" Aunt Lola asked.

"She drove the car into the ditch a couple of weeks ago," Dad said.

Uncle Abe's eye widened. "Were the kids in the car?"

"No, I only had Molly along," Mom said. "The others were in school. I laid her on the front seat so I could keep an eye on her as I drove. When I came to the top of a hill, I saw a car coming halfway in my lane so I swerved to my side of the road, hit a patch of loose gravel and flipped into a steep ditch."

"Oh, my goodness!" Aunt Lola pressed a hand to her chest.

"Yeah, it's a miracle they didn't git hurt a lot worse," Dad said. "Even with her broken arm, Gladys picked up Molly and walked a half mile to a farmhouse to call for help."

"Did Molly git hurt?" Aunt Lola asked.

"The doctor said she had a concussion," Mom said. "We had to watch her carefully for a few days, but she seems okay now."

"That's good." Aunt Lola looked relieved. She motioned toward the front door. "Now come on in the house. I made coffee and fresh cinnamon buns for you."

I ran into the house ahead of the others. I wanted one of those cinnamon buns before my brothers snitched them all.

～

When Molly was barely a year old, Mom drove all of us kids to town to buy groceries. Usually she went while we attended school during the day, but this was in the summer.

As Mom got out of the car, she said, "You kids stay here. I'll be back in a few minutes."

The last thing I wanted was to be locked up in a hot car with Clyde. I clutched the back of the seat. "Aw, Mom, can't we come with you?"

"There ain't no way I'm draggin' three kids and a baby into the store. We'd be in there all day. Now you stay here and be good. I'll be back soon. Roll down the windows so you don't git too hot."

Clyde and Jimmy opened all of the windows. Molly started to cry as soon as the door slammed behind my mother. I climbed into the front seat, hugged her and tried to comfort her, but she kept bawling.

Clyde flopped his arms over the back of the seat and leaned toward us. "Mommy ain't comin' back. She's left us here all by ourselves."

"Don't tell her that," I said.

"Yeah, you dummy." Jimmy whacked him on the arm. "You're makin' it worse."

Clyde kept at it, "Mommy ain't comin' back. Mommy ain't comin' back." Molly cried all the harder.

I started to sing her favorite song to cheer her up. "Mary had a little lamb, little lamb, little lamb." She hugged her dolly, listened to my silly song and smiled at me. We touched noses, and I patted her cheeks.

"Mommy will come back soon," I said.

Suddenly, Jimmy stuck out his arm and pointed. "Hey, look at that new car—a 1951 Ford. Ain't that a beauty?"

"I ain't never seen one that purdy either," Clyde said. The boys knew every make and model of car on the market.

"A red and white convertible," I said. "I wish we could see him put the top down."

We all stared at it. After the man dropped his letter in the mailbox, he came back and started putting the top down. We watched with wide eyes and dropped jaws.

First, he unzipped the rear window and unlatched the header. He pressed a button inside the car to start lifting the top. It stopped at the halfway point. He adjusted the material and tucked it all in the proper place. Then he pushed the button again, and it lowered all the way. He snapped the trim in place, climbed in and took off.

"Wow!" I said. "I ain't never seen nuthin' like that."

"I wish I had one of them." Jimmy's eyes widened.

Mom came back to find us still admiring the convertible. She put her paper bags of groceries in the trunk, and then opened the door to pick up Molly. When Mom shrieked, we all spun our heads in her direction to see what was wrong. Mom clutched the bottle of one hundred pink baby aspirins that she'd bought earlier that day. She shook the bottle and a couple of pills fell out. Molly had traces of pink around her lips. She smiled angelically at us. Mom's face turned pale, then red with anger.

"Why didn't you kids watch her?"

"We were. I didn't see her doing nothin'," I said.

Mom jumped behind the wheel and drove like a maniac to the Schuyler Memorial Hospital. She parked the car in the parking lot, grabbed Molly and headed for the emergency entrance. Clyde, Jimmy and I scurried into the hospital behind her.

When Mom told the intake nurse what happened, she immediately escorted her to have Molly's stomach pumped out.

The rest of us sat in the waiting room. "It's your fault, Lizzy. You should have watched her," Clyde said.

"I *was* watching her." I threw my hands into the air. "I'm only seven. Why didn't you or Jimmy see her? You're bigger."

I already felt horrible. Clyde's words made me feel even worse.

When I saw Mom trudging down the hallway, clutching Molly to her, I raced toward them and hugged my little sister. "Is she gonna to be okay?"

"Yeah, the doctor said it was a close call, but they cleaned out her stomach," Mom said. "Thank God, we discovered it right away."

That incident scared me half to death. I could have lost my beautiful sister. I had to be more watchful. I renewed my resolve to keep an eye on her.

~

A few months later, I decided to teach Molly how to walk. "Okay, Molly, let's go walk, walk," I said.

"Walk, walk," she said.

I remembered seeing my aunt teaching my cousin how to walk by holding an empty one-gallon Karo syrup pail in each hand, so I tried it with Molly. I placed her against a wall and beckoned for her to come to me. Whenever she fell down, I helped her balance again, until she could walk on her own. She toddled around and around, much to our family's delight.

"Molly, you can walk!"

"Walk, walk." She dropped the pails and clapped her hands.

Later that day, when Mom rocked her to sleep, I stood on the side of the rocking chair with one foot at the back of the runner and the other at the front. That way I could rock them both without any effort on their part. I listened to Mom sing to her and watched her cuddle Molly as she fell asleep. I always wished someone would hold me and rock me.

Do only babies get to be loved? I need hugs, too.

Within a few minutes, Mom would say, "Okay, that's enough of that. She ain't never gonna git to sleep with you standing there."

I leaned over and kissed Molly on the cheek. "Night-night, Molly."

She smiled back at me with her big brown eyes. "Night-night, Wizzy."

≈

When Molly was three years old, she became seriously ill. Mom and Dad had worried about her body temperature being high during the night. At dinner the next day, as she sat in her high chair between my parents, she started to wobble and passed out.

Dad called the doctor in Schuyler, and he came to our house to check on her. When his attempts to help her didn't work, he asked my mother to bundle her up. He drove both of them to the Columbus hospital, where he discovered she had double pneumonia.

That frightened me. What was going to happen to my little sister? Would she die? When would Mom come back home?

Mom stayed with Molly at the hospital until she recovered. I jumped for joy the day Dad went to pick them up. When I came home from school, there was Molly.

"Molly, you're back! I missed you so much." I hugged her so tightly, she squeaked.

"I wub you, Wizzy," she said.

"I love you, too, you little squirt."

≈

A year later, at age four, she became critically ill again. She had been coughing and had a high fever.

"Quick, wrap her in a blanket!" Dad said. "We're taking her to the doctor."

Clyde, Jimmy and I put on our jackets and headed out the door. Mom wrapped Molly in a couple of warm blankets and raced to the car.

We lived seventeen miles from Schuyler, the nearest hospital and the town where our doctor practiced. Dad drove faster than he normally did on those gravel roads, but it still seemed like it took forever to reach it.

Mom cried. I could hear her praying, "Oh, God, don't let her die!"

I clasped my trembling hands together in my lap and prayed, too.

When we reached the doctor's office, Mom and Dad took Molly inside. The doctor examined her and gave her some medication and we started for home. About two miles down the road, Molly went into convulsions. It scared the heck out of me. I started shaking. My stomach knotted up so tightly I could hardly breathe. *Is Molly dying? What would I do without my sweet sister?*

Dad turned the car around and rushed back to the doctor's office. The doctor said he suspected something serious and raced off to the hospital with us following close behind him.

After the doctor had examined Molly, he returned to the waiting room where Dad, Clyde, Jimmy and I waited.

"I did a spinal tap on Molly. She has spinal meningitis," he said. "You'll have to take the other children back to my office and have them vaccinated, so they don't contract it, too."

Molly remained quarantined in the hospital for five days. Mom stayed with her. If life was chaotic with Mom at home, it proved much worse when she wasn't. Dad had never learned to cook, but he managed to make us oatmeal for breakfast. Clyde and Jimmy helped make the sandwiches for our lunch pails, even though they cut the bread slices way too thick. Dad fried eggs for dinner. We skipped our weekly baths.

I worried day and night about my baby sister.

Dear God, please help Molly to git well.

When Molly returned home, she had to stay in bed for another week. I could barely believe she was still alive. While Mom returned to her household duties, I played with Molly. I hugged her and she hugged me back. I held her and rocked her. I sang her favorite song, *Mary Had a Little Lamb,* over and over, except I said *her* name instead of "Mary." Her eyes started to sparkle again.

"I love you, Molly."

"I wub you too." She patted my cheek.

I held her on my lap facing me, tucked her chubby little hands into mine and gave her a bumpy ride, "Humpty Dumpty sat on a wall. Humpty Dumpty had a great fall." At the end of that line in the poem, I dropped her down between my knees.

She laughed and said, "More, more." I tired out long before she stopped asking for more.

That illness scared our family, but it became only one of many more trips to emergency. Every time Molly's temperature became elevated, like the times she broke out with measles or chicken pox, she started having convulsions. It terrified me to see her shaking. I always feared she would die.

When she was still four, Molly had her tonsils removed. A year later she had an emergency appendectomy. Not long after that, she rolled out of bed in the night and broke her collarbone. She had her arm in a sling for the next six weeks.

Clearly, my sister was in for a rough ride through life. I watched her sleep as I stood beside her bed one night. Moonlight streamed through the window and fell across her face so that she almost glowed, like an angel. My fists clenched. Molly might have a lot of trouble in life, but I vowed, in that moment, that I would do everything I could to watch over her and protect her. Nothing was going to hurt her ever again, not if I could help it.

V

Hello, Grandma!

WE LOVED TO VISIT GRANDPA AND GRANDMA LEWIS, MY MOTHER'S parents. They lived in a small house in Columbus. Grandpa, a short and round little man, had sparse white hair and wore spectacles. Grandma used to have red hair, before it turned gray. She weighed a bit more than she should have and walked a little hunched over. She always wore Hush Puppy shoes that made next to no noise when she walked. But her laugh was loud and contagious.

Now and again Grandpa would let out a loud "Whiskey" when he sneezed.

"Oh, for cryin' in a bucket, Grandpa!" she said. "Stop that. It's not good for these kids to hear words like that."

"But Grandma, we like the way he sneezes," Jimmy said.

"Yeah, it's funny," I agreed.

"Well, wouldn't that frost your buttons?" she said. "Now he'll never change."

Whenever we went to their house, Grandma gave each of us a Hershey's chocolate bar. Our parents seldom bought us candy, so that was a special treat. Once Grandma opened a bar for Clyde and held it out to him. He took one giant bite and gobbled half of it at once. Grandma looked surprised. "Well, ain't that the berries?" Then she chuckled so hard she almost fell off her chair.

≈

In the early 1950s, Grandpa retired from the Union Pacific Railroad, and he and Grandma moved to Minnesota. We could never visit them there, but Grandma wrote to us about it and sent us photos.

They lived by a small lake surrounded by thousands of birch trees. Grandpa loved to fish in the lake beside their house. In the winter, he cut holes in the ice to catch them.

Grandma told us about the deer that walked through their woods and the cute chipmunks that ate right out of her hands. We wished we could go there and see all these amazing things, but they lived 500 miles away.

Grandma sent us a card for each of our birthdays. She had over twenty grandchildren, but she remembered us each year until we went to high school. We could hardly wait to open it.

"Wow! Grandma sent me a whole dollar," I hollered. "I can buy lots of things with this."

Other than the money we received from Mom for good grades on our report cards, that was the only cash we saw all year.

Our grandparents came to Nebraska to visit us once each summer for a week or two. We fought over who would sit beside them at mealtime.

"I want to sit by Grandma," I said.

"No, it's my turn," Molly said.

"I have two sides, girls," Grandma said. "One of you can sit on each side."

Grandpa told funny jokes to make us laugh. Grandma gave us many much-needed hugs. We hated to see them leave.

Once in a while Grandma would call our family from Minnesota. Mom would answer and then give us each a quick minute to greet her. She always laughed when she heard our voices.

"Hi, Grandma!" I said.

"How are you doing in school?" she asked.

"Real good. I got all A's on my last report card."

"That's my girl! Keep up the good work. I love you."
"I love you, too, Grandma. I miss you."

≈

Our telephone was on a party line with nineteen other neighbors. We heard everyone's phone ring, which the company distinguished by a combination of long and short rings. Our number was 9083, and our ring—two longs and two shorts.

We got in trouble from our parents if we lifted the receiver and listened in on someone else's conversation. Besides, the ladies seemed to know when someone sneaked into their conversation, and they'd say, "Hey, get off the line!"

If we had an emergency, and someone else was on the line, all my dad had to do was pick up the phone and holler, "Hello! This is Clarence Bauman. We have a sick baby here. Could you please git off the line so we can call a doctor?"

The other party would comply immediately.

We were not allowed to make telephone calls, not even to our friends. Telephones were for emergencies. I would be at least sixteen before I made my first personal call. I had to have help doing it, because I had no idea how to dial the operator and ask her to connect me to the number I wanted. Long-distance calls cost several dollars for a few minutes, so they were out of the question.

No one talked on the line during a thunderstorm. If lightning struck a telephone pole only a half-mile away, it would blast the transformers above our phone into smithereens. We'd find pieces of them all over the room.

≈

If lightning storms terrified me, imagine what the treat of tornados instilled in me. Dad had a good eye for watching for bad weather. We lived in "tornado alley" and had to be on constant guard for them.

Suddenly, the wind would pick up, the clouds would roll in, and we had to head for cover.

When Dad heard of a storm warning over the radio, he stayed up after his regular bedtime of 8:00 p.m. to watch for tornados headed our way. When he spotted one, he hollered, "Git in the cellar!"

We came pounding down the stairs. Mom and all of us children headed for the primitive cellar under our farmhouse. After we dashed outside and down the dirt steps, Dad closed the rickety old wooden door. We waited and trembled.

"How long do we have to stay in here?" I asked.

"Quiet!" he said. "I'll let you know when you can leave."

We had no light down there, except for the flickering flame of a kerosene lamp, and then only if Dad had taken the time to grab one. The damp clay floor and walls felt clammy and unpleasant. The musty smell irritated my nose. Along one wall, I could see shelves of jars with fruit and vegetables that Mom had canned from her garden. A huge bin of potatoes, freshly dug from the garden patch, filled one corner. Without them, we would perish from hunger in the winter.

We had no place to sit down, so we stood there in the dark. I shivered and shook. The loud rumbling roar of the wind terrified me. I started crying, but no one reached out to comfort me. Dad held on to the door of our cave and peeked out now and again to see if it had gone past. Mom cradled my little sister Molly, who whimpered incessantly.

My brother Clyde seemed unaware of the gravity of the situation and made fun of my fears. "Don't be such a crybaby," he said.

Jimmy finally put his arm around me. "It's okay," he said. "Don't be afraid. God will protect us. The storm will soon pass." I buried my head in his shoulder and felt somewhat comforted.

When Dad deemed it safe to leave the cellar, he sent us all back to bed.

Jimmy took my hand and led me out of the cellar and back to my bedroom. I had a hard time going to sleep.

What if another tornado comes while we're sleeping?

I prayed the prayer I learned in Sunday school:

"Now I lay me down to sleep,

31

I pray the Lord my soul to keep.
If I should die before I wake,
I pray the Lord my soul to take."

That prayer troubled me. Why would I die before morning? Would a tornado strike our home and wipe us out? Would I be involved in an accident? Would I become sick? If God loved me, why wouldn't he protect me? These thoughts chased around inside my head like a couple of squirrels in a walnut tree.

VI

Recess at School

MY EARLIEST MEMORIES OF CLYDE'S TORTURE TOOK PLACE DURING MY Kindergarten year at our one-room school in Howells, District 11. One chilly day, while we played outside on the playground, the teacher asked Clyde to fill a bucket with water and bring it in for the students to drink. He was a big kid in the fifth grade. I followed him to the well and watched him pump the handle up and down to fill it. Only the big kids were strong enough to do it. Then, without warning, he dumped the whole pail of cold water over my head. After a moment of shock, I rushed screaming to the teacher.

"What happened?" Miss Richter asked.

"Clyde dumped cold water on me."

"Clyde, why in the heck did you do that? Go to the library, and I'll deal with you later."

He shuffled off to the library.

Miss Richter peeled off my wet dress and put her own jacket on me to keep me warm.

"You can wear this until your clothes dry," she said.

My cheeks burned with embarrassment, but she dried my tears and talked calmly to me. She hung my clothes over a chair near the furnace grate in the floor of the main classroom. Her kindness surprised me.

I wish she was this nice all the time.

Clyde probably received punishment for what he did that day, but I don't remember what. You didn't want to cross Miss Richter.

Did Jimmy see what happened? Will he tell Dad? Should I tell? I wished he would receive a second punishment, like I always did. But then, he would retaliate, and I'd be even worse off. I'll stay out of his way the next time we go out for recess.

≈

The teacher allowed us to go outside for fifteen minutes each morning and afternoon. All of the students, from Kindergarten to the eighth grade, played together. In good weather, we played softball. I don't think I ever made it safely to first base. The ball beat me there every time, and I got sent me back to the batting lineup.

One time, my brother Clyde pitched a softball to one of the other older students. She hit it straight into his face and broke his glasses.

"Oh, no!" she said. "I'm sorry. Did I hurt you?"

His nose bled all over his shirt.

"You broke my glasses," he said. "Now I won't be able to see, and we ain't got no money to buy new ones."

Several of the older students bent down and looked for the pieces in the grass. I saw the girl who hit him with her hands folded and her head bowed. She must have been praying.

"I'll talk to my dad," she said, when she looked up. "He'll probably pay for them."

That ended the game.

Serves him right, the old bully. But he gits free new glasses. How does he rate?

We played other games at recess. For one of our favorites, steal the cobs, we drew a line in the dirt. Two captains each picked the kids they wanted on their team.

"I'll take Lizzy," Joseph said. "She's fast."

"I'll take Daniel," the other captain said. "He's sneaky."

They always picked Clyde last. No one wanted him on their team.

We all lined up at the centerline. Each side had a pile of ten corncobs placed about twenty feet behind the line. After someone hollered "Go," we had to break through the opponent's line, grab one of their cobs and make it back to our own pile without being tagged.

I waited a moment, then raced over and grabbed one while the other team chased the bigger kids.

"Way to go, Lizzy!" Joseph hollered. "Watch that sneaky Daniel."

Whichever team stole all the other's cobs first, won the game.

Our schoolyard had little equipment for the sixteen students to play on—only a slide and a few swings. We younger ones asked the older girls to give us a push until we learned how to do it ourselves. One day, Clyde walked by and grabbed my swing. He hauled it back as far as he could, then let go and pushed it hard. I started to scream. He laughed and pushed it again.

"Stop, Clyde! Stop!" I shouted.

Laurie, one of the bigger girls, pushed him away and slowed me down so I wouldn't fall. I got off the swing, tears streaming down my face.

"Leave the little kids alone, you big bully," she said.

He stomped off, but not before he glared at me. "Scaredy-cat."

I didn't like the slide at all. Sometimes I got up the nerve to slowly inch my way up the ladder to the top. Then I would sit down, hang on tightly to both edges and let myself slide only a few inches at a time.

One day, I climbed up the slide one last time just as Miss Richter rang the bell for classes to begin again. This time I was more afraid of being late than of hurting myself, and I zipped right down.

Hey, that was fun!

VII

Holidays

WITH CHRISTMAS COMING UP SOON, JIMMY AND I STARTED WISHING FOR what we'd like to receive. He had turned ten and I was eight.

"I want some new shirts and a Tinker Toy set," he said.

"I want a brand new dress and a book of cut-out dolls." I reached for a pencil on the table. "I'll put a dolly with eyes that open and shut on Molly's list. I think she'd like that."

"Do you think we'll actually git these?"

"Probably not, but it's fun to wish anyway."

We each wrote a list on lined white paper. Mine was longer than Jimmy's.

"Do you think there's really a Santa Claus?" I asked.

"Well, if there is, he don't know where *we* live," he said.

"Yeah, I thought so."

We scrunched up our lists and threw them in the wastebasket.

≈

Each year, right before Christmas, Dad, Clyde and Jimmy went out into the woods and cut down a small, scraggly fir tree. Mom, Molly and I decorated it with a few handmade ornaments. We made popcorn and threaded it onto a string for garlands. I colored and cut a yellow star out of paper for the top of the tree. Molly made a few circles on paper, colored them and cut them. Mom tied a piece of thread on each one to hang from the branches.

That year, Dad set the tree in the middle of the floor and told us to join hands and form a circle around it. He sang, *Oh, Tannenbaum,* as we walked slowly around it. We laughed and tried to sing along. We didn't know the words to the song, but we relished the feeling of happiness for a few minutes. It must have been a tradition from when he was a child. But we never did it again.

Christmas has always been one of my favorite holidays, even though we received few gifts. My parents had about ten dollars to spend on the whole family. If we received a new toothbrush or a pair of socks, we had to be content with that.

That particular Christmas, I ripped the paper off my gift. "Wow! Look what I got—paper dolls!" *Kathy sometimes lets me play with hers when I go to her house after school. I put them on my Christmas list, but I didn't expect to ever have my own.* "That's exactly what I wished for." I held them up for everyone to see. "Thanks, Mom."

Clyde received a shiny pocketknife. He smiled and slipped it into his pocket.

Molly opened her gift and discovered a doll with eyes that opened and closed. She squealed with delight.

"One of the deacons at church gave me a few dollars to buy you kids some gifts," Mom said.

"Tell them 'thank you' from us," Jimmy said. "I didn't expect a Tinker Toy set."

I leaned over and whispered in Jimmy's ear. "Maybe there *is* a Santa Claus."

"Or else Mom found our lists in the wastebasket," he said.

Jimmy built impressive designs with his Tinker Toys, while I punched out each doll and her clothes. I dressed them over and over by bending the tabs on the shoulders and sides.

Hello, pretty little girl. Which dress do you want to wear today? The pink one? Okay. I wish I had nice things to wear like you do.

≈

Our church put on a Christmas pageant every year. The director often chose me to be Mary. I felt special to have been picked to portray that quiet and gentle soul because, deep in my heart, I felt like that, too. I held on to that little Baby Jesus as if he were my own tiny sibling.

After the program ended, the deacons handed out bags of candy, fruit and nuts to all the children. I guarded mine carefully so my brothers wouldn't take my goodies.

"Keep your grubby hands off my candy."

"I ain't touchin' your stuff."

I traded some of my soft chocolates for Molly's hard candy, so she wouldn't choke on them.

"Here, these are better for you, Sis."

"Thank you." She gave me a hug.

≈

We always looked forward to the visit from my father's two older brothers, Friedrich and Heinrich, and their wives every Christmas. Neither couple had children of their own, so they arrived from Columbus bringing our family oranges, hard candies, chocolate 'haystacks' and other goodies. On occasion, they even brought a ham. I loved to open the Navel oranges and see if I could find a small slice in between the larger ones.

"Look, Jimmy! I have two babies in my 'belly button' orange."

"Lucky you. I only have one," he said.

We devoured the chocolates in a hurry. We sucked on hard candy for days after Christmas. What a feast!

≈

We usually had fried chicken for Christmas dinner, or ham, if our uncles had brought one. One particular year, Mom decided to prepare something different.

On Christmas Day, after we said grace, Mom brought a roasted bird to the table. Dad carved pieces for each of us. Clyde wanted a drumstick. Jimmy, Molly and I asked for some white meat. It tasted different from the chicken we usually ate.

"What kind of meat is this?" Jimmy asked.

Mom looked a bit sheepish and hesitated before answering. "It's goose."

"Goose?" We all choked and spit out the bite in our mouth.

"You didn't kill Goosie, did you?" I looked at her in dismay.

"I'm afraid so." She stuck her hands into her apron pockets.

Jimmy pushed the meat aside on his plate. "I ain't eatin' him."

"Me neither." I pressed my hand to my mouth so I wouldn't barf.

Clyde kept right on eating.

I tried to keep the tears from coming until I left the table. How could we eat our pet? We had hatched him from an egg our Aunt Lola gave us. When we called, "Here, Goosie, Goosie!" he would follow us all around the farm, looking for a handout of grain. And now Mom had killed him. How could she?

After we had washed the dishes, Jimmy said, "I ain't never eatin' goose again, as long as I live."

"Me, neither," I said. I had a sick feeling in my stomach the rest of the day from the few bites I did eat.

≈

In a rare display of sympathy, Dad offered to take Jimmy and me for a sled ride after dinner. We put on our coats and boots and followed him outside. A few inches of freshly-fallen snow covered the pasture close to the house. Dad tied the sleds to the back bumper of the car and said, "Hang on!"

He didn't drive fast, but we went much faster than if someone was pulling us by hand. Wet snow from the tires flew into our faces, so we covered them as well as we could with one hand, while clinging to the sled with the other. We zipped around and around for a few minutes.

"That was fun! Thanks for the ride, Dad."

"Yeah, thanks Dad. We should do this more often." Then Jimmy put the sled back in the barn.

It helped us forget our sadness at the dinner table.

Dad sure was nice to us this afternoon. I wish he were that nice all the time.

VIII

Our Family's Religion

MY PARENTS PRACTICED THEIR RELIGION AT HOME AND MADE US FOLLOW some strict rules. They attended Baptist churches before they married, but since our community only had a small Presbyterian church about a mile and a half from home, we went there. Everyone spent an hour in Sunday school and then another in the worship service, unless, of course, we had a high fever, had recently thrown up or had broken out with some dreaded disease.

One Sunday, Mrs. Petracek, my friend Kathy's mother, taught us a lesson on the Ten Commandments in Sunday school. She had attached two large hand-drawn stone tablets to a flannel background. She had written a children's version of the commandments on separate strips of flannel so she could add each one as she talked about them.

She gave us each a drawing of Moses holding two tablets of stone with the numbers one to ten on it. "If you don't obey these, your heart will become black and you will need to have God clean it," she said.

This is good. I'll have a list of things not to do so I can keep my heart clean.

I opened my box of crayons and made sure they were in the right order—red, blue, yellow, green, orange, purple, brown and black. I *always* kept them in that order.

Mrs. Petracek placed the first strip on to the flannel background and smoothed it. "The first commandment is 'We must love God more than anything or anyone else.'"

I put up my hand. "More than my kitten Sylvester?"

"Yes, a lot more," she said.

I outlined the stones with the brown crayon.

She added another strip. "Second, God wants us to worship only him and not make anything more important than him."

"I guess that means no lucky rabbit's foot?" one youngster said.

Mrs. Petracek ignored that comment and continued. "Third, always use God's name with love and respect."

"My dad always says, 'Oh, my God!'" one youngster said.

"And my mom says, 'Oh, my Lord!'" another added. "Is that okay?"

"That would be breaking the third commandment," Mrs. Petracek said. "If we love him, we should respect him and not quote his name foolishly."

I colored Moses' cloak blue and his sash red.

She smoothed another strip on to the tablets. "The fourth commandment says we should work six days and keep God's seventh day special. That's what we do on Sunday, although the Jewish people do it on Saturday."

"Is that why you won't let us do anything on Sunday, Mom?" Kathy asked.

Mrs. Petracek let out a huff of annoyance.

"The fifth commandment is 'Love and respect your Mom and Dad.'"

I looked up from my coloring. "Even if they spank me with the strap?"

"If you obeyed them, they wouldn't have a reason to strap you, would they?" she asked.

"I guess not." I tried to think that one through, as I drew a yellow sun in the top right corner of the picture.

Mrs. Petracek swiped her hand over another strip. "The sixth one is not to hurt another person."

"My brother Clyde punches me, and sometimes it hurts somethin' awful."

"Then his heart will turn black."

That I could believe. I drew a black rock in the bottom left corner and pretended it was Clyde's heart.

"The seventh commandment is for your moms and dads to be faithful to each other, like they promised at their wedding."

One little guy started to say something, but his big brother clasped his hand over his mouth.

"The eighth one says, 'Don't steal.' If it's not yours, don't take it."

"If you borrow something and don't give it back, is that stealin'?" a little girl asked.

"Yes, it is. So be sure to return everything you borrow, especially money."

I tried to think if I had disobeyed that one. I drew a few tufts of green grass around Moses' feet and the rock.

"The ninth one is 'Do not lie.' We should always tell the truth."

I gripped the green crayon tightly. "Is it okay to tell a lie if you know you're gonna git a beatin' for tellin' the truth?"

"That would be a hard decision to make, but the right thing to do is to tell the truth."

I wonder how many times I've lied? No wonder my heart is so full of black spots.

Mrs. Petracek placed the last strip onto the tablets. "The tenth commandment is, 'Don't wish you had something others have.' You should be happy with what you have."

There are a lot of things I wish I had like Kathy and Nancy—new shoes, pretty dresses, a television. They're so lucky not to be poor like we are.

Before Mrs. Petracek dismissed the class, she gave each of us a list of the Ten Commandments and reminded us to obey them at home. I carefully returned all my crayons to their proper spot in the box. When I arrived home, I pulled an old piece of chewing gum off my painted and chipped metal bed frame and stuck Moses and his commandments on the wall close by.

I took my new autograph book, the one Kathy had given me last Christmas, out of my dresser and wrote on the first page:

Things I shouldn't do so Dad doesn't whip me,
and so I don't get dark spots in my heart.

~

One of Dad's rules stated that girls couldn't wear 'men's clothes.' That meant that I could never wear anything that covered my legs, like slacks or jeans. If he ever caught me doing so, he would whip me, like the day I didn't remove my snow pants at school.

One day I asked him, "Where'd you git that rule?"

"It's in the Bible," he said.

"Where?" I thought he might be making it up.

It took him a long time, but he found it in Deuteronomy 22:5. "A woman must not wear men's clothing, nor a man wear women's clothing, for the Lord your God detests anyone who does this."

"Don't that beat all? It's in there," I said.

If I wear men's clothes, God detests me? That's frightening. It's scary enough to offend my father, who can actually whip me. Is God like that? Is he out to git me for every little thing I do wrong? I don't want to find out.

I added that to the list in my book:

Don't wear boys' clothes.

~

My parents had an unshakeable respect for the Bible, not only the contents, but also the actual book. They never allowed us to put anything on top of it. More than once they caught us setting the Sunday 'funnies' on one.

"Who in the Sam Hill laid the newspaper on this Bible?" Dad yelled. "This is God's Holy Word. You don't set nothin' on top of it."

"I saw Clyde reading it." I shrank back against the wall.

"Not me, you dummy," he said. "Jimmy had it last."

"Jimmy, was that you?"

"Maybe. I'll be more careful next time."

"You'd better be, or I'm gonna tan you."

≈

The verse Dad quoted most often was, "Spare the rod and spoil the child." As he beat us, he would say, "My kids ain't gonna be spoiled." I hated that verse, but I thought he had a right to beat us if he wanted to. He had God to back him up on that one.

God, couldn't you have provided better methods of keeping us from going astray? Why'd you tell him to beat us?

Dad disciplined us without mercy. My mother had no sympathy for me when I received a beating. My parents had never heard of a "time out." It was only "game over."

≈

My mother also punished us if she heard us swear. She considered "dang" as bad as "damn," a word Jimmy and I pushed to the limit one day. As we played, we talked about the beavers in the creek building a *dam*. We babbled on and on, using *dam* in every sentence we could. Finally, it reached Mom's ears.

"Who's swearin' in there? Do you want your mouth worshed out with soap?"

"We ain't swearin'," Jimmy said. "We's talkin' about a beaver dam."

I whispered in Jimmy's ear. "She's got *dang* good hearing."

We could have argued that Dad said, "Sam Hill," "tarnation," and some German swearwords, but we didn't dare.

I wrote in my book:

Don't never swear.

≈

Dad also said, "Children are to be seen and not heard." He prohibited loud chatter around the dinner table. We could ask to have food passed to us, but he allowed no arguing or complaining. As a result, I always spoke in a quiet voice.

One day I raised my hand to ask Miss Richter a question. "Could I go to the library and find a book to read?" I whispered.

"What'd you say, Lizzy?"

"I want to go to the library and get a book," I whispered again.

"Lizzy, you have to speak up, or I'll never know what you want."

After several attempts, I dissolved into tears.

If I talk loud, I feel like I'm yellin'. With yellin' comes spankings. I don't understand all these stupid rules, but I have nowhere else to go. I have to live here until I'm eighteen, so I'd better start learnin' to obey better.

That night I read over the lengthy list in my book and determined in my heart to be more obedient. After I crawled into bed, I said my prayers. *God, please help me to obey all those rules.*

Maybe tomorrow would be less stressful. I would at least try to be good. I also hoped I could find a way to get rid of the growing collection of dark spots in my heart. They were starting to hurt badly.

≈

The church I attended gave an altar call at the end of each service. If someone felt convicted by what the pastor had said, or if they had a burden to share, he or she could go up to the front of the church. There the minister would listen to their confession and pray for them.

The song they used most often during this time was, *Just As I Am.* They started to sing . . .

Just as I am, without one plea,
But that thy blood was shed for me,
And that thou bid'st me come to thee,
O Lamb of God, I come, I come.

As I thought about going to the altar, questions whizzed through my mind. I wish someone could help rid me of these bad feelings. The pastor said God could make my heart clean again. How does he do that? I learned in Sunday school that Jesus died for my sins, but I've tried asking him before and it didn't work. Will it this time? Maybe God is angry with me and wants to punish me, like my daddy does.

I stared at my feet, bit my lower lip and started to quiver. I'm only eight years old, but I'm already such a bad person. I feel dirty—permanently stained.

I hesitated as long as I could. The congregation started singing the second verse . . .

Just as I am, and waiting not
To rid my soul of one dark blot,
To thee whose blood can cleanse each spot,
O Lamb of God, I come, I come.

That's it! I have one dark blot—no, lots of dark blots. But how can I rid myself of them? Can Jesus make my heart clean?

After the second verse, I walked slowly to the front. Tears streamed down my cheeks. I wiped them away with my sleeve and dropped to my knees in front of the pastor.

He knelt beside me. "What's the matter, Lizzy?"

"I'm bad. I have lots of dark spots in my heart." I burst into tears again.

"Can you tell me what caused the dark spots?"

"I . . . I . . . I can't."

I listened as the congregation continued on with another verse.

Just as I am, though tossed about
With many a conflict, many a doubt,
Fighting and fears within, without,
O Lamb of God, I come, I come.

Fears? That's something I know. My family is Christian, but no one knows what's happening inside our house. And nobody can do anything about it—not even God. I would run away if I could, but I have nowhere to go.

The pastor prayed for me while I continued to weep.

"Lord, bless Lizzy. Forgive her sin. Wash away the dark spots in her heart. Give her peace. Amen."

The pastor gave me a tissue and patted me on the shoulder. "I hope you'll feel better now."

I wiped my eyes, blew my nose, took a deep breath and trudged to the back of the church. Peace didn't come. I took my burdens back home with me and continued to carry them around in my heart. Why could no one help me?

IX

My Father

I TRIED TO FIGURE MY FATHER OUT, BUT MY THOUGHTS TOOK SO MANY twists and turns that I never learned what made him tick. As soon as I started to feel safe around him, I would do something to make him angry and he would punish me.

My dad worked all his life as a farm laborer for a hundred and fifty dollars a month, except when he served in the army. When he went into the service, Clyde had recently turned five, Jimmy two and a half and I was barely seven months old. Dad served for nine months, from March of 1945 until shortly before Christmas. My mom said I was afraid of him when he came back. Can you blame me? He had been gone most of my life.

He always wore a faded blue long-sleeved shirt and striped bibbed overalls, made by the Key Company. He often tucked his thumbs behind the buckles of the straps. He carried a flat yellow carpenter's pencil in the front pocket. While six feet tall, he only weighed about 150 pounds.

Dad came from a large family of ten children. Two other brothers with the same name, Clarence, died in infancy. He came somewhere in the middle. His oldest sister raised him after his mother died giving birth to her thirteenth child. Dad was only eleven.

Dad spoke only German at home until his mom died. Then they changed to English, as his father was a second-generation immigrant, but his mother a first-generation. He told us about an incident when he had trouble translating the time of day from English, which he knew from school, to German for his mother. One day as she worked in the garden, she asked him what time it was. He ran to the house, looked at the clock, which showed 2:30, came back and told her it was "halb zwei" instead of "halb drei." (Half two, instead of half three.) His dad gave him a beating for telling a lie.

We learned about Dad's home when we visited his siblings, who related tales of horror from their childhood. They told how Grandpa Bauman beat some of his children so badly, he almost killed them. He even beat the horses on the farm, when they wouldn't do what he told them. We seldom saw him as we grew up.

≈

In 1949, when we moved from Columbus to Howells, Dad's boss put him in charge of hundreds of acres of farmland. He grew corn, barley and wheat for the market and clover for cattle food. He worked long, hard hours in the fields. He also fed a herd of twenty-five white-faced Red Angus cattle, which he eventually sold to the market for beef. He had a few Holstein milk cows, which provided our family with milk, cream and butter. He sold the rest to the creamery. The profits went to his boss, not us.

Dad went to bed at 8:00 p.m., as he had to get up early the next morning to milk the cows. "It's time to hit the hay," he'd say. "Now you kids git to bed. If I hear any noise up there, I'm comin' up with the strap." We would race upstairs and climb under the covers. We didn't dare protest or beg for a glass of water. Bedtime was *not* negotiable.

≈

Just after I turned five in 1949, my Grandpa Bauman became seriously ill. Our parents couldn't leave us alone at home so many miles away from Columbus, so they took us along to the hospital. He was lying in bed with a white sheet over him. Someone knew he liked cold wieners and had brought him some. I watched him rocking from side to side as he munched on them.

Before we left, the family gathered around his bed and sang, "Jesus Loves Me," to him. I thought that was a song for little kids, but he sure liked it. He thanked us, and we left.

Not long after that, he died, and we attended his funeral. The only thing I remember is that my brown shoelace came untied during the service. Dad reached down and tied it. He had never dressed me or done anything that kind for me before. It stuck in my mind. I looked up at him and smiled.

Why can't people always be as nice as they are at funerals?

≈

Dad worked at least fourteen hours a day, six days a week. He milked the cows every day at 4:30 a.m. and 4:30 p.m. We could never leave the farm for more than a few hours. If we ever took a trip, it was on Sunday afternoon to visit one of Mom's or Dad's siblings and our cousins. Omaha, Nebraska, about 100 miles away, was the furthest I ever went from home as a child, and that was only once every few years.

No trip to Disneyland, which opened in 1955. No swimming in the ocean. No sightseeing at the Grand Canyon, Mount Rushmore or the Statue of Liberty. My whole life centered within an area of about thirty miles from home—Howells, Schuyler, Genoa and Columbus. We had a lot of relatives living in the latter, as both of my parents grew up in that city.

Dad drove us in our 1933 Chevy. Mom sat in the front with Molly on her lap. Clyde, Jimmy and I sat in the back. To drive the thirty miles to Columbus took almost an hour. Gravel roads made the journey treacherous, so Dad took it easy.

We played a game called "bury the horses" as we drove along. We counted how many of them we could find in the pastures along the road. If we passed a cemetery, we had to "bury" them and start over. After a while, if you got smart, you learned which side of the road had the fewest cemeteries and claimed that part of the back seat on the way home.

We also loved the Burma Shave signs. The company wrote their advertisement on a half dozen or so signs and put them at intervals along the highway. We tried to see who could read them first. Here are some examples.

Past Schoolhouses
Take it slow
Let the little
Shavers grow
Burma-Shave

Train approaching
Whistle squealing
Stop
Avoid that run-down feeling
Burma-Shave

Keep well
To the right
Of the oncoming car
Get your close shaves
From the half pound jar
Burma-Shave

We also played a game where we tried to find each letter of the alphabet on a sign or license plate. Whoever found "Z" first, won.

This game produced a few squabbles, though.

"You didn't really find the 'Q' already. You must have cheated."

"No, I didn't. I saw it on a Quaker oil sign."

Gas cost about twenty-eight cents a gallon in the 1950s, so we had to use it sparingly. Our old car could only drive ten to twelve miles per gallon. A trip to Columbus and back would cost two dollars. That was a sizable chunk out of Dad's one hundred and fifty-dollar monthly salary. The grocery list would have to be shorter the next week.

On the way home from an afternoon visit in Columbus, Dad drove down a steep hill that had an intersection near the bottom. A car tearing along the other road roared right through the stop sign.

Dad slammed on the brakes and yelled, "Darn fool!" We slid to a halt as the other car whizzed in front of us. The abrupt stop threw me into the front seat. Jimmy banged his head on the window. Clyde had braced himself for the impact, so he was okay. Molly bumped her head on the dashboard, even though Mom had a tight grip on her.

"He coulda killed all of us," Dad said.

"If I find out who he is, I'll take care of him." Clyde clenched both his fists.

That night I prayed again, "If I should die before I wake, I pray the Lord my soul to take."

I almost did die today, God. Thank you for protecting my family and me. Keep us safe from harm—and I mean here at home, too.

≈

The next day I learned that God *does* protect little girls. Our family had finished the noon meal, fried potatoes with ketchup smeared on them. Mom picked up my baby sister Molly and sat in the rocking chair. She sang to her as Molly drifted off to sleep. Dad stretched out on the linoleum floor face down with his arms under his head for his afternoon nap. He had milked the cows and worked in the fields all morning. He needed a rest before going back to hoe sunflowers out of the cornfield.

Clyde, Jimmy, and I wandered down to the barn to play cards in the hayloft while he slept. No one dared wake him in the middle of his nap. We left the dishes unwashed on the kitchen table.

We played with a deck of Crazy Eight cards. Mom wouldn't let us use the ordinary cards, the ones with the King, Queen, and Jack on them. "Them's from the Devil," she said. "Don't let me ever catch you usin' those."

After about half an hour, I heard Mom calling from the house up the hill, "Lizzy, git yourself up here and worsh the dishes."

I ignored her. I could always say I couldn't hear her from that far away.

She called a second time, but again I pretended not to hear. We had played a few rounds, when one of my brothers put his finger to his lips and said, "Shh."

We heard stealthy footsteps on the barn stairs. Dad! I felt paralyzed. My heart raced and I started to tremble.

"Quick, jump out the loft door!" Clyde pointed toward the opening.

"I can't. It's way too far down," I whispered.

"He'll beat you," Jimmy said.

It took all the courage in my heart, plus a lot more, to crawl over to the edge of the doorway, turn around backwards and hang by my fingertips until my little feet touched the gate below.

He's gonna beat the heck out of me. I gotta git out of here. God, help me.

I jumped off the gate and scrambled as fast as I could go. When I reached the house, I could barely breathe.

"Why didn't you come when I called you?" Mom planted both fists on her hips.

"I didn't hear you."

Oops! That's a lie—another black spot in my heart.

"I sent Dad down to look for you. Did you see him?"

"Nope."

"Git these dishes worshed up before he comes back."

I quickly filled two dishpans with hot water from the reservoir in the end of our cob-burning kitchen stove. In the middle of drying them with shaking hands, Dad returned to the house.

"You're lucky I didn't catch you up in the barn," he said. "I would have tanned your hide."

I shook for a long time after that. I thought about my narrow escape and wondered how I had ever made it out of the loft without getting hurt. When I prayed my little prayer that night, I thanked God for helping me escape from the barn and avoid another beating. That incident became the fuel that kindled many nightmares.

My Father

I wrote in my little book:

Go wash the dishes when Mom calls,
and don't lie that I didn't hear.

X

My Mother

I WANTED MY MOTHER TO HUG ME, TO LISTEN TO ME WHEN I WAS IN trouble and to protect me from anyone who tried to hurt me. I could wish all I wanted but, "If wishes were horses, beggars would ride."

Mom stood barely five feet tall and ended up a bit round in the middle from all her pregnancies. She had a thin face, long brown straggly hair and brown eyes that often stared off into space. She had to work hard and had few resources to make her job easier.

Mom took her religious faith seriously. She and Dad attended church regularly and made sure we did, too. She liked to help her ladies' group with their mission projects, like ripping old sheets into three-inch strips and rolling them.

"Do you want to help me?"

"Sure, but why are you doin' this?"

"The missionaries use these for bandages for the lepers in Africa." She handed me a strip to roll up.

"What are lepers?" I started rolling one long strip.

"It's a contagious disease that causes some people not to be able to feel pain. Sometimes they even lose their fingers or toes because they don't realize they're hurtin' themselves when they touch somethin' hot."

She showed me a brochure she had brought home with photos of people with leprosy.

"Oh, that's horrible!" I said.

She also showed me pictures of black children from Africa.

"Holy Smoke! I ain't never seen no people with black skin."

"That's because most of the people around here came from Europe, where they's white."

"Like Great-Grandpa Bauman from Germany?"

"Yes."

We finished rolling the strips and put them in a box to take to church. Soon they would be on their way to Africa.

≈

Mom baked bread every couple of days so we'd have something to eat in our school lunches. She had so many other things to do that she didn't always take time to knead the dough long enough—the loaves had giant air holes in them. The jam leaked through and made a huge mess. At least she made an effort to feed us.

If Dad happened to be away, Mom led the mealtime prayers. Unlike Dad, she prayed and prayed and prayed—for the missionaries, for the lepers in Africa, for the sick, for the pastor and his family, for all sorts of needs around the world, before finally thanking God for the food.

Every so often Jimmy and I would peek up to see if she would finish soon. Jimmy grabbed a slice of bread and hid it in his lap. He smiled. Emboldened by this, I snitched one, too. The next time I looked over at him, he put his finger through a hole in his piece and wiggled it at me like a little worm. That struck my funny bone, and I exploded with a snort.

Mom stopped in the middle of a sentence and looked up at us.

"What are you kids doin'?" she asked. "Did you start eatin' while I was prayin'?"

"Mom, you shouldn't pray so long," Jimmy said. "We're hungry, and the food gits cold."

"Oh, all right," she said, "but you should wait until I finish."

After lunch, I walked upstairs and wrote in my book:

If I ever have kids, I'm gonna say short mealtime prayers.
And don't snitch no more while Mom is praying.

57

≈

Mom kept the finances for our family and paid the utility and doctor's bills, even if it took months or years to pay them off. She kept track of our expenses in a lined notebook. My parents believed in tithing, giving ten percent of their income back to God, so she made sure we gave away fifteen dollars of our meager income each month to our church and missions.

"Why do you give away that money, when we need it to buy groceries?" I asked.

"It's our way of saying 'thank you' to God for providing for us," she said.

I wrote in my book:

Learn to give back to God.

≈

She also saved green stamps, which she received from buying groceries. We had to lick them and stick them in little booklets. When she had filled several of them, she redeemed them for merchandise.

Jimmy and I looked through the green stamp catalogue to see what we could trade them for.

"I'd like a new doll."

"I'd like a toy car."

When we told Mom what we wanted, she said, "No toys. We need towels. The ones we got ain't fit for rags."

"All that lickin' stamps for a couple of towels?" I asked Jimmy.

"Oh, well, maybe we'll git to use 'em the next time we take a bath."

≈

Mom sewed some of our clothes. The rest came from other people's castoffs. We seldom had anything new from the store, except for shoes. When the time came for us to buy a new pair, she set a piece of paper or cardboard on the floor and said, "Stand still while I draw around your foot." Whoever needed shoes took a turn.

"I want saddle shoes, like Kathy's, the white ones with a black strip across the middle," I said.

"You'll git whatever I can afford to buy," she said.

She took the drawing to the store, picked out new shoes for us and brought them home. We didn't always like them, but we could either wear them or go barefoot. Sometimes she bought them out of the Sears and Roebuck catalogue, in which case we had a choice of what color and shape we wanted.

≈

Washday on the farm presented a challenge for my mother. On Saturdays, she started the process early in the day. First, someone had to carry several pails of water in from the well across the farm, if it hadn't rained lately to fill the cistern. We dumped a bit of water down the spout of the pump to prime it, and then pushed the handle like crazy until the bucket filled. We tried not to splash too much out as we struggled back to the house with our load.

Mom poured ten gallons into the reservoir of the kitchen cob-burning stove. She also filled an oval-shaped aluminum tub on top of the stove. It took a long time to heat up that much water. One of us had to stoke the stove with dried corncobs every few minutes, so the fire stayed hot. The cobs gave off a strong sweet odor. They also let off a bit of smoke, which attached itself to the giant cobwebs in the corners of every room.

Mom and I searched through the bedrooms, brought all the dirty clothes down and sorted them into piles on the kitchen floor—whites, colors, darks. Thankfully, we didn't have to use a scrub board, as we had an electric washing machine with a wringer.

When the water was hot, she filled the machine, added some powdered soap and started through the piles of laundry. She washed each load for a few minutes. Then she put the clothes through the wringer to squeeze most of the dirty water out of them.

"You watch them clothes as they come through the other side, so they don't get wrapped around the roller," she said.

"I'm afraid I'll git my fingers caught."

"Just do it, and stop complainin'."

The clothes fell into a tub of cold, clean water, where she swished them around for a bit and then sent them through the wringer a second time. They next went into a clothes basket.

"Go hang them on the line," she said. "I'll come and help you after I start the next load."

I grabbed the bag of clothespins and a basket of wet clothes and began to hang them on the clothesline in the side yard of the house. In the summer it wasn't too bad of a job, but winter nearly killed me. My fingertips turned to icicles, and then the clothes did the same. My dad's frozen long johns looked hilarious flapping in the wind. When the stiffness blew out of them, we knew they had dried. We had to fetch them back off the line and put them away.

I loved to sniff the clean, dry laundry. It smelled like a whole field of wildflowers.

≈

We took a bath every Saturday night, whether we needed one or not. Mom set the round aluminum tub in the middle of the kitchen floor and put in a couple of inches of warm water from the stove reservoir. The boys were old enough to bathe themselves, but mom still scrubbed me, as I was only eight.

"I ain't goin' in Clyde's dirty water," I said.

"Then you'll have to wait until I warm some more," she said. She dumped his dirty water out the front door.

Lucky Kathy has warm water right out of a faucet—and a nice bathtub, too.

As I grew older, I washed my hair over the tiny kitchen sink. We rinsed it with white vinegar mixed in the water. It made my hair squeaky-clean. When I was young, Mom put curlers in my hair and let it dry overnight. It hurt my head to lie on them, but in the morning, I had ringlets like Shirley Temple.

≈

Mom never would have won an award for the world's best driver. On one of the rare occasions when she took us shopping, she couldn't back out of her parking spot. After several attempts, she rolled down the window and asked a guy on the street to do it. She jumped out, let him drive out, and then climbed back in. Another time the motor caught on fire in front of a store. As Mom sat helpless in the car, someone noticed the flames and came out to douse them with a bucket of water.

If she had to drive up a hill and stop at the top before turning left or right, she could never make it on the first try. She would let the car roll backwards a ways, then take another run at it. It didn't help matters that Clyde hollered at her how to do it, while Molly screamed her head off.

"Gosh, Jimmy, I don't think we're gonna make it," I whispered.

"Me neither."

We both sat holding our breath and clutching the doorknob. When we finally turned onto the road, we let out a little cheer.

One blustery cold day, she tried to start the car to drive us to school. After several attempts to turn the key, she twisted it too hard and broke it off in the ignition.

"Damn it!" she said.

Jimmy and I gasped and stared at each other with our mouths wide open. She would have washed ours out with soap for saying that.

"I'll run to the house and find another key," Jimmy said.

Clyde found needle-nosed pliers in the barn, gripped the bit of key still sticking out and removed it. Jimmy gave the other key to her. After a bit of fiddling, the car finally started. We arrived at school ten minutes late. Clyde explained to Miss Richter what happened so she didn't give us any detentions.

≈

Neither would Mom have ever won an award for the world's best housekeeper. Our house always looked like a cyclone had whipped through it. If Dad came home extra tired from working in the field and noticed the mess, he would holler, "What ya' been doin' all day, Woman? This house looks like a pigsty. It's a fire hazard."

She would grab the broom, start sweeping and put a few things out of sight. When she cleaned, she gave the house "a lick and a promise." Only, she usually didn't keep her promise to do it better the next time. She did the absolute minimum of good housekeeping, and sometimes far less.

~

I tried to please my mother by helping her clean and do the laundry, but I despaired of getting her to like me any more than before. I thought getting good grades in school would make her proud of me, but it only made things worse amongst us siblings. I decided to keep trying, even though it seemed hopeless. Maybe something would work someday.

XI

My Brother Clyde

IF I COULD HAVE BRAIN SURGERY AND HAVE THE MEMORIES OF ONE person removed permanently from my head, it would be those of my oldest brother Clyde, who was five years older than I. He had a "burr in his tail" for as long as I can remember. Not only did Clyde mistreat me, but also some of the animals on our farm. We had a pet dog named Buster, a cross between a German shepherd and a collie, with a handsome black and white coat. He followed us everywhere. He proudly presented himself in every family picture, panting and smiling from ear to ear.

My parents didn't allow animals in the house, so Buster slept in the back porch. He could open the screen door by himself. He had many mishaps over the years. Giant hailstones broke his back once and he sat at the end of the sidewalk and howled. Jimmy and I took some water and food over to him, as Buster couldn't walk for a long time. He licked our faces in appreciation.

Another time Dad ran over him accidentally with the front wheels of the tractor. Jimmy and I stroked his coat and brought him scraps to eat. We never took him to a vet, as our parents could barely afford to take us children to a doctor.

One day, Clyde decided out of the blue to rub some turpentine, used for cleaning paint brushes, on Buster's behind. He howled and tore around the farm like a crazy dog until it wore off. Clyde laughed—Jimmy and I didn't. We tried to catch him and wash it off.

"Don't you dare tell Mom or Dad about this, or I'll beat you to a pulp," he said.

After he walked away, Jimmy said, "If his brains were dynamite, he wouldn't have enough to blow his nose."[2]

Even though we laughed at him, we knew Clyde could carry out his threats, so we kept quiet.

When Buster finally settled down, I put my arms around his neck, hugged him tightly and said, "I'm sorry, Buster. That ol' Clyde is meaner than a settin' hen."

He licked my cheek.

"Your coat stinks, but your heart smells good." I gave him another hug. He reciprocated with more slobbery licks.

≈

We also had numerous cats that lived in the barn to keep down the mouse population. When the mother cat gave birth to a new batch of kittens, we each claimed one for our own. Jimmy chose a black one with a white spot under its chin and four white paws. He named him "Boots." Mine was the opposite, mostly white with a few black markings on one ear and the tip of his tail. I named him Sylvester. His fur felt so soft. I carried him with me all over the farm. When I petted him, he purred so hard, he made me laugh. "You're the perfect kitten, Sylvester." We loved to watch our special kittens play tag with the other ones in the barn. We had so much fun with them.

Jimmy and I used to scratch Sylvester's ears, which made him shake his head. We asked him questions to see if he would answer "yes" or "no." If I asked, "Do you like Jimmy?" I'd scratch him softly so he wouldn't respond. If I asked, "Do you like Clyde?" I'd scratch him extra hard to make sure he said, "No." If that didn't work, I blew on his ear. Then he would do it for sure. It's amazing what information you can wriggle out of a kitten.

≈

One day, when I was playing with Sylvester and the other kittens by myself in the hayloft, Clyde came up the stairs and sat down on the bale of hay beside me. Without saying a word, he slipped his hand under my dress.

"Hey, what are you doing?" I tried to squirm away.

"I'm just tickling you."

I jumped off the bale of hay to run to the house. I turned and saw a weird look on his face. I had no idea what he had done to me, or why my body felt the way it did. I wished Sylvester could answer that one for me, but I wouldn't even have known what questions to ask.

≈

Mom bought a hundred baby chicks each spring. She housed them in a little coop on the east side of the house, where she fed them and kept them warm until they were old enough to go outside in a small pen. During the day, they wandered all around the farm. At night, they stayed in the coop.

We had a larger barn on the west side of the house for the chickens after they had outgrown the coop. My dad had nailed strips of boards across the inside back of it for them to roost at night. On the opposite side, he made several rows of stacked wooden boxes about 18" square then stuffed them with hay where the hens laid their eggs.

The roof of the building slanted downward from front to back, so we could easily climb up and sit on it. One day Clyde started pulling the protective caps off the roofing nails.

"Look, guys, it's easy."

Jimmy and I pulled a bunch off, too. Soon each of us had a pile of them. The next time it rained, the roof leaked like a sieve and soaked the chickens.

"Who did this?" Dad asked.

"Jimmy and Lizzy."

"Clyde showed us how."

Dad went into a rage. "What in tarnation would make you hoodlums do a thing like that? There are a thousand leaks in that roof now. Do you want me to lose my job for destroying the chicken coop?"

"No."

Dad stomped off to the back porch and brought the strap. He started with Clyde, the obvious ringleader. Whack! Whack! Whack!

It sure is good to see Clyde get a lickin' once in a while.

When Dad finished with him, he started on Jimmy. Whack! Whack! Whack!

Maybe he'll run out of steam by the time he gets to me.

He hadn't. Whack! Whack! Whack! It felt like I got one wallop for every cap we pulled off the roof.

"If I lose my job," he said, "I'm gonna whip all of you again."

Before the next rain, Dad made Clyde replace all the nails in the roof. Clyde had to pay for them out of his own money. That made him furious. He stomped his feet and screamed at Jimmy. "I'll learn you to snitch on me." Then he picked up an aluminum cake pan from the kitchen table and slammed it down on Jimmy's head. It bent right in half. Jimmy howled with pain. I fled upstairs.

It's too bad our parents didn't see it happen, but Mom did wonder how her pan came to be in such pathetic shape. No one would say a word. We knew now what Clyde meant when he warned us not to squeal on him.

≈

Clyde kept to himself most of the time. One day Jimmy and I caught him smoking some weeds he found in the woods. He did it on the sly so our parents wouldn't catch him at it. When he offered them to us, we walked away, because we knew that would mean big trouble. He kept his stash in an abandoned stove out among the trees behind the house. He threatened us with impending doom if we told our parents.

≈

Jimmy and I liked things cleaner than the rest of the family. One day we swept the sidewalk between the house and the outhouse. It looked great for a change. Not long after that, I noticed Clyde had dumped wagonloads of dirt on it.

"Mom, Clyde dumped dirt on the clean sidewalk!" I screamed.

"Now what'd you go and do that for?" she asked.

"Because I felt like it," he said.

Through my tears, I swept it all again. Jimmy helped.

"He acts like he's got a cob stuck up his butt all the time, don't he?" Jimmy said. [3]

"Yeah." I wiped my tears and chuckled at that thought.

≈

One day Jimmy and I played with our kittens, watching them chase a piece of string on the front porch. Clyde came along with an old car tire from the barn and said, "Want to have some fun?" He demonstrated how to give it a shove and roll it down the hill.

"Whoever catches it first gits to bring it back up and take a turn," he said. It provided a bit of diversion on a boring summer day. After a while, I became hot chasing it down the hill and rolling it back up for my turn.

Clyde noticed Sylvester wandering between my ankles. He picked him up and said, "Want to go for a ride, Kitty?"

"No, don't do that to my kitten!" I screamed.

"It won't hurt him none," he said.

"Don't do that!" Jimmy yelled.

Clyde didn't listen. He stuffed that ball of white fluff into the tire, gave it a shove and laughed as it rolled down the hill. "Go, Kitty!"

Jimmy and I ran as fast as we could so the tire wouldn't roll so far. Jimmy caught it just as it stopped rolling and plunked over. He gently pulled Sylvester out of the tire and handed him to me. I held him for a long time. When I set him on the ground, he stumbled, and then tried to stand up again. I picked him up again and cradled him in my arms. A few minutes later, he died while I held him.

"Breathe, Sylvester, breathe."

"He ain't gonna breathe no more," Clyde said. "He's dead."

"You killed my kitten!"

I picked up a handful of dirt and threw it at him.

"Oh, well, there's more in the barn. Go pick one of those."

"But I loved Sylvester more than any of the others."

"Too bad."

Jimmy came over to comfort me. I sniffled. "He killed my bestest kitten."

"I'm sorry," Jimmy said. "Do you want to bury him behind the house?"

"Okay." I picked up his already stiff little body.

Jimmy found an old shoebox. I went to my room and found one of my favorite doll blankets, a white one with pink hearts on it. I wrapped little Sylvester in it and closed the lid. Tears streamed down my cheeks as I watched Jimmy dig a hole large enough to bury the box.

Before I set it in the hole, I took one more peek inside the box and stroked Sylvester's soft fur.

"Good-bye, little Sylvester. I love you. I'll miss hearing you purr."

We put the box in the hole and covered it with dirt. Then we found a piece of cardboard and wrote, "Sylvester, Lizzy's pet kitty," on it. We attached it to a stick and put it near the grave. For a long time afterwards, I cried every time I passed his burial spot. My heart was in that box.

≈

Things continued to grow worse at home. Clyde threatened to kill me if I ever told anyone about him touching me, so I kept quiet. The dark spots in my heart multiplied. I began to feel so dirty. Did anyone care?

My bedtime prayer, "If I should die before I wake," often became a sincere pleading for my life, after a rough day of living with Clyde's threats.

XII

My Brother Jimmy

JIMMY, MY OLDER BROTHER BY JUST TWENTY MONTHS, BEAMED RAYS OF sunshine into my dark world. On rainy days, he spread a rainbow in my sky.

The summer I turned seven, we often played in the woods behind the house. We planted pretend crops by bunching up piles of dirt and then harvested them into grain piles, like our Dad did on the farm. We could reap several crops in one morning. Our grain bins overflowed with corn and wheat.

Jimmy piled up a heap of dirt. "Ol' Mr. Franklin is gonna be happy with this year's corn crop."

"Yeah, he's gonna have to build more silos," I said. "Look at all this wheat."

"Better git that hay into the barn before it rains."

"I hope there ain't no tornadoes comin'," I said. "Watch them clouds."

We used old empty Band-Aid cans for cars and tractors. We used marbles for our pretend people. We named them after our dad's boss and our family.

Mom hollered from the house. "Dinner is ready."

"Let's go," Jimmy said. "I'm so hungry, I could eat half a cow."

"Me, too."

≈

Jimmy claimed he had several compartments in his stomach, like a cow. If we had more than one item to eat for a meal, as for Sunday dinner, he would eat all of his potatoes first, then all of his fried chicken, then the vegetables. He wouldn't allow the different food groups to touch on his plate. If he ever spilled something on his shirt, he changed it right after the meal.

≈

We only had one working 26" girls' bicycle for the three of us older children to share. I asked Jimmy to teach me how to ride it after I turned seven. I was so small I couldn't sit on the seat, so I stood on the pedals. We took the bike out to the end of the driveway and faced it downhill on the gravel road.

Jimmy held on to the back fender, while I tried to keep my feet on the pedals.

"Okay, give me a push," I said.

Jimmy pushed. I rode a short distance and fell over.

"Let's try this again. Don't let go. Keep hangin' on to me."

Jimmy pushed and ran along behind me as I zipped down the hill. After wobbling quite a ways, I hollered, "Stop! Stop!"

Jimmy didn't stop me.

"Help! You forgot to show me how to use the brakes."

About a quarter of a mile later, the bike finally slowed and I flopped to the road. I looked back and saw Jimmy standing near the top of the hill. I thought he had been beside me all that time.

"Hey, I can ride all by myself!" I pushed the bike back to the top of the hill, climbed on and zipped down again.

Piece of cake.

Nothing could stop me from riding after that. Jimmy and I built ramps with narrow boards and flew over them. We didn't always make it, but we had fun trying. Later, when someone gave us a second old clunker, we rode together. One time when we went for a ride, Jimmy decided to take the left fork in the road on the way back, and I the right. Then we both changed our minds at the same time. We crashed and landed in a heap. My leg started to bleed, so he wiped it with his hanky. We rode home to clean and bandage it. It was nice to have one person in my life who took care of me and cared when I got hurt.

≈

Sometimes Clyde played with us, too, but when he did, we always had to abide by his rules. One day the three of us decided to play softball behind the house. Clyde wanted to practice his pitching so he could do it better at school. He pitched, Jimmy caught and I batted. One day I didn't do what he told me to, so he threw the ball hard at my head. I didn't even see it coming. I instantly dropped to the ground, unconscious.

When I came to and felt my throbbing head, Jimmy helped me up. I stumbled to the house. Clyde had disappeared.

When we entered the house, Mom clasped her hand over her mouth. "What happened to Lizzy?"

"Clyde threw a ball at her and hit her in the head." Jimmy helped me over to a kitchen chair.

Mom's eyes narrowed. "Was it an accident?"

"No, he got mad at me, 'cause I didn't stand the way he wanted me to," I said.

She gave me a cold washcloth to put on my goose egg and went to find Clyde. She found him sitting on the front porch. "Why'd you hurt Lizzy?"

"She don't never listen to me when I tell her how to play ball."

"That don't give you no excuse to hurt her though. I might tell Dad what you did."

"You'd better not." He stomped off.

Mom never told Dad, and Dad didn't seem to notice the purple bruise on my temple.

≈

Since we lived beside a gravel road, every couple of years the county maintenance people came and added another layer to it. Then Jimmy and I would go stone hunting. We collected the prettiest pieces of gravel and took them back to the house. I kept my collection in a hole in a hollow tree. One day, as I attempted to retrieve some of them to play with, my arm got stuck in the hole. I sent Jimmy to the house to fetch our mother.

"What's goin' on here? What'd you do?"

"My arm is stuck. I tried to git my stones back out of the tree."

"Stones? What in the devil are they doin' in a tree?"

"Where else was I supposed to hide them?"

She tugged and pulled on my arm, but couldn't free me.

"Ow, it hurts!" I yelled.

"Why were you so crazy to stick your arm in that small of a hole?"

"My prettiest stones are in there. I want them back."

Mom brought a kettle of water and a bar of soap out of the house to loosen my arm. She slowly inched it out. I had a few scratches, but at least I didn't have to spend the rest of my life with it stuck in a tree—my right arm, to boot.

≈

I tried to outperform Clyde and Jimmy at everything they did. One day they decided to see who had the best sense of balance. They walked along the narrow metal frame of a farm disc, a piece of machinery with sharp flat blades for breaking up the clods of dirt after the spring plowing. When my turn came, I confidently stepped onto the bar and started to walk along it. Suddenly, I lost my balance, fell forward and banged my forehead on the metal crossbar.

Clyde laughed. "Serves you right."

Jimmy came running. "Are you okay?"

"No, my head hurts."

"You have a big 'goose egg,'" he said. "Let's go to the house and put some cold water on it. You're lucky you didn't fall on one of them sharp discs."

"Thanks. This is bad enough."

~

We used to make up crazy songs to make each other laugh. We had a teacher named Miss Schuster, so we sang:

Schuster, Schuster, married a rooster.
Rooster died, Schuster cried.
Schuster had to marry another rooster.

After several more verses, we laughed until we almost peed our pants. Then we made up yet another verse:

Roaster, Roaster, married a toaster.
Toaster died, roaster cried.
Roaster had to marry another toaster.

We could laugh all we wanted at home, but laughing in church didn't bode well for us. The next Sunday Jimmy and I sat on the right side of Dad on the church bench. Our feet didn't reach the floor, so we entertained ourselves by swinging them back and forth.

Dad frowned and laid his large weathered hand on my leg. We stopped kicking our feet.

After a few minutes, Jimmy leaned over and whispered, "Doggie, doggie, married a foggy," and let out a snicker. His laugh was far more contagious than the chicken pox. I sniggered in response.

Dad gave us a stern look. We took a deep breath and turned away from each other to collect our thoughts. We clamped our lips shut, and for good measure pressed our fists against our mouths. Unfortunately, as we repeated and embellished the rhyme in our minds, it became even more hilarious. I took one peek at Jimmy, and when I saw the twinkle in his eyes, we both burst out laughing again.

Dad whispered, "Wait 'til you two git home!"

That sobered us. We knew what that meant. Thoughts of getting strapped have a way of erasing funny things.

XIII

My Classmates

I SHOULD HAVE LEARNED TO KEEP MY TONGUE IN MY MOUTH, BUT I didn't. One day, after most of the students had gone out for recess, Miss Richter reprimanded me for sharpening my pencil too often.

"You only want an excuse to run around the classroom," she said.

I felt that was untrue, as I only wanted my pencil sharp for making neat letters in my penmanship book, so I stuck my tongue out at her.

It's one thing to do that to a brother at home, but you didn't dare do that at school. That meant *big* trouble.

"Okay, Lizzy, I'm sending a note home to your parents to tell them what a disrespectful child you are."

I plopped my head down on my desk and started to weep.

She came over, squatted to my level and asked, "What's the matter? Why are you crying?"

"My daddy will beat me when he gits that note."

"You know how disrespectful it is to stick your tongue out at someone, don't you?"

"Yes, I'm sorry. I'll never do it again."

After my tearful apology, she relented and decided not to send the note home. Luckily, my brothers weren't in the room at the time, or they would have snitched on me. Nancy and Kathy each grabbed one of my hands and took me outside to play on the swings.

I loved school and all my subjects—math, handwriting, reading and English. I even liked geography, although I had a problem getting the earth oriented properly in my mind. The desks in our schoolroom faced east, and I must have missed the lesson when we learned that the top of every map was north, so the top of my world felt like east to me. It totally screwed up my sense of direction.

One day, the teacher assigned us the poem *Trees* to memorize. I took a copy of it home and worked like crazy on it. The next day, when our turn came up, the teacher asked us to recite it. Kathy and Nancy tried and tried, but could only say the first few lines.

"Well, Lizzy, what about you?" she asked.

I took a deep breath, stood stiffly with my hands behind my back and recited the whole poem, almost without stumbling.

> *I think that I shall never see*
> *A poem lovely as a tree.*
>
> *A tree whose hungry mouth is pressed*
> *Against the sweet earth's flowing breast;*
>
> *A tree that looks at God all day,*
> *And lifts her leafy arms to pray;*
>
> *A tree that may in summer wear*
> *A nest of robins in her hair;*
>
> *Upon whose bosom snow has lain;*
> *Who intimately lives with rain.*
>
> *Poems are made by fools like me,*
> *But only God can make a tree.*

"Joyce Kilmer wrote that."

"Excellent!" Miss Richter said.

She praised me! That feels so good. Maybe I could do that again. I like poetry. Maybe I'll write some of my own.

≈

After a couple of hours of classes, we stopped for lunch. Kathy and Nancy picked up their fancy square lunch buckets with Roy Rogers and Dale Evans on one and Snow White and the seven dwarfs on the other. I grabbed my shiny Karo syrup pail and sat with them on the cement front steps of the school to eat.

"What do you have today?" Kathy asked.

"A jelly sandwich." I took a big bite.

"That's the same as you've had all week," she said.

"I know. What's in your lunchbox?" I peeked over at hers.

"A meat and cheese sandwich and one of Mom's sweet rolls."

"Oh, lucky you!" I said. "That would be so yummy."

"I have a roast beef sandwich and some apple pie," Nancy said. "They're leftovers from last night's supper."

It sure would be nice to have a lunch like that once in a while.

After we finished our lunches, we all drank water from the enamel dipper, and then plunked it back into the pail. We raced over to the yard to play for the rest of the noon break.

≈

"You can stop by my house after school," Kathy said. "Mom said it was okay."

"That would be fun. I'll tell Jimmy I'm comin' home later."

Kathy lived on a farm between our house and the school. Sometimes my parents allowed me to visit there after school. Her parents came from Czechoslovakia. Mrs. Petracek was an excellent cook and baker. Every so often she made fresh "kolaches" for us to eat after school. Those delicious pastries, filled with fruit and topped with

77

icing, tasted heavenly to me. She only let us eat one, though, so we wouldn't spoil our appetite for supper.

I loved their spotless house—so different from our messy one. They even had an indoor bathroom. Their pneumatic player piano in the parlor, which Kathy's mom allowed me to look at, fascinated me the most. Mrs. Petracek showed me one of the large scrolls of paper with holes punched in them. Then she inserted it into the piano. When she pumped the pedals, it played the most beautiful music I had ever heard.

"What the dickens?" I said. "I ain't never heard nothin' like this. It sounds like there's a little guy inside that there piano, playin' his heart out."

Mr. Petracek, a kind and witty man, winked. "Maybe there is."

I also saw my first television at their house. Not many people had them yet in the early 1950s. The Petraceks, well-to-do farmers, could afford such things.

At supper that night, Clyde announced the news. "Joseph Petracek said his dad bought one of them newfangled televisions."

"We ain't never gonna buy one though, even if we did have the money," Dad said. "If you have one of those, you're invitin' the Devil right into your living room."

I gulped and clenched my mouth shut with my fist. Kathy and I had watched a program after school.

Devils in a television? What about the ones who are already running loose in this house?

≈

When Molly turned five, she started Kindergarten. Dad fitted a seat on the back of my bicycle, so I could ride her to school. On that first day, she couldn't balance well, so I wobbled all over the road, up and down the hills for two miles.

"Hang on, Molly," I said.

"Don't go too fast." She wrapped both arms around my waist and squeezed tightly. "It scares me."

"Stop wigglin', or you're gonna make me spill."

She whimpered most of the way. I complained that I had to carry such a heavy load at only eleven years of age. I shook from exhaustion by the time we arrived. Later, Jimmy would sometimes trade bicycles with me and carry her. Clyde attended high school in a small town nearby, so he couldn't help.

I watched over Molly at recess, accompanied her to the outhouse if she needed to go, and pushed her on the swings, but never too high. At home, I practiced printing the alphabet with her. I read her stories and helped her learn to read from her *Dick and Jane* books.

"Look, Jane, look. See Spot run," she read. She looked up at me and grinned.

"Hey, you're a good reader," I said. "Read the next page, too."

When she finished, we found a box of crayons and started coloring together at the kitchen table.

"What's your favorite color?" I asked.

"Pink." She smiled. "What's yours?"

"Green. I'm a green monster, and I'm gonna tickle you," I said.

She giggled so hard, she almost fell off her chair.

However, even with all my help, Molly struggled in school. The concussion from the car accident, the many illnesses and the seizures made it difficult for her. She needed much encouragement to keep learning.

≈

One day in the sixth grade, Kathy, Nancy and I chatted in the basement of the school during recess. Even though we were all eleven years old, they had both matured much sooner than I had. They decided to mention that trivial fact to me.

"Hey, I got boobies already," Nancy said.

"So do I," Kathy said.

"How about you, Lizzy?" Nancy asked.

"Nope. I ain't got nothin' yet." I crossed my arms over my flat chest.

"I'll show you mine, if you show me yours," Nancy said.

"I told you already. I ain't got nothin' to see," I said.

They pulled the neckline of their shirts down until I could indeed see what they had. That made quite an impression on my pre-teen mind.

"Come on, Lizzy, it's your turn," Kathy said.

I reluctantly showed them my bare, flat chest.

"Why, you ain't got nothin' but fried eggs," Nancy said.

"I told you so." My face turned red. Now I had one more reason to feel ashamed of my body.

Will I ever grow nice boobies like my friends have? I'm eleven. Why do I still look like a boy? Hurry up, Mother Nature! You're shirkin' on the job.

XIV

Moving to Clarks

IN 1955, WHEN I WAS ELEVEN, MY MOTHER MISCARRIED TWO MORE BABIES. When she was about to miscarry the second one, she sent me down to the barn to fetch my dad.

"Mom says she needs you real quick," I said.

He seemed to know what I was talking about, without an explanation. He went running like crazy to the house to help her, but it was too late. It surprised me to see him care so much about what was happening.

Later that week, Dad lost the job he'd had for the past six years. I never learned why. I had only seen him cry once before, but that must have been the last straw for him. I hid in my room and prayed.

What's gonna happen to our family now? We can barely survive when he has a job. God, please help my dad find another job.

He went to the employment office and soon found another farmhand job near a little town called Clarks, with a population of about 450 people. We had to move.

I hugged my friends Nancy and Kathy on my last day of school there. We all cried.

"You'll write to me, won't you?" I asked.

"Sure," Kathy said.

"But you'll have to write first," Nancy said, "because we don't know your new address."

"Okay, I'll send it to you." I made sure I had their correct addresses.

≈

My parents sent Molly and me to our Aunt Lola and Uncle Abe's home for moving week. Clyde and Jimmy stayed to help. They didn't allow me to pick out the clothes and toys I wanted to take along to our new home. I'm not sure who packed or how they transported everything to the new house.

Aunt Lola had a difficult time with Molly as she cried the whole week. My aunt carried her around and tried to calm her by singing to her. Sometimes it worked. Sometimes it didn't.

Aunt Lola taught me a few new things while I stayed there. She showed me how to fold towels in thirds, then in half twice. They stacked well that way.

She taught me how to iron clothes. Even though I was eleven, I had never done that. For one thing, when I plugged the iron into the wall socket at our house, the sparks that arced from it frightened me. The iron also took a long time to heat up and I wasn't patient enough to wait.

When the time came for my aunt and uncle to drive us to our new home, I became so excited. What would my new room be like? Had they brought along my dollhouse and toys? Maybe Molly would finally stop crying.

When we arrived, my mom gave me a hug, which she rarely did. I ran upstairs to my room. It was small, with space for only a bed and a dresser. A naked light bulb hung from the ceiling. It had a string attached from the pull chain to the bedpost, so I could turn it off without getting out of bed. It would be good enough for Molly and me to sleep in.

"Where's my doll house?" I asked.

"We didn't have no room to bring all that stuff," Mom said. "We left it at the other house."

"What? How could you leave my favorite things there?" I yelled. I stomped outside. Moving to a new place started off badly.

The next day, a school bus picked us up at our farm and took us to our classes in town. I had more students in my sixth grade class than in my whole school out in the country. My teacher, Mrs. Slovak, an elderly lady nearing retirement, had a distinct shade of blue-rinse gray hair.

She was kind and welcomed me. She encouraged the other students to do the same.

Some said, "Hi, Lizzy."

I felt so scared, like I didn't belong here. When Mrs. Slovak wasn't watching, some of the kids pointed at me and made fun of my frumpy clothes.

I wrote to Kathy and Nancy and told them I had over twenty students in my sixth grade class. I told them how much I missed them. I didn't think I'd ever make new friends like them.

Even though I had come from a little country school, I wasn't far behind in my studies. Things went well, until the spring when I suddenly became ill with whooping cough. My teacher sent home my assignments with my brother Jimmy so I could finish my studies and go on to the seventh grade. I passed, even though I missed the last six weeks of school.

Whooping cough nearly killed me. After I coughed until I vomited, I couldn't breathe back in. I made a long rasping sound. It felt like I was going to choke to death.

Clyde yelled at me whenever it happened. "Stop doing that."

"I can't help it. I can't breathe."

"Yes, you can." He punched me in the back every time he heard me do it.

Mom spoke up for me and told Clyde I really had no control over the whooping. I'd had the same disease at three months of age. She said she had to hold me upside down and pat me on the back to make me to breathe again. That must have been scary for her—and me. I was relieved when I received my report card that year, and found out I had passed.

Drawing done in the seventh grade

~

I had a wonderful teacher in the seventh grade, Mrs. Croft, who taught us how to draw. One day she took our class outside and had us sketch a barren tree. She said she could hardly believe how real mine looked. She also put artwork on the blackboard for us to copy—a still life scene with fall vegetables. I couldn't see it from my desk, so I continually walked up to check out what to draw next.

Mrs. Croft noticed my dilemma and notified my parents that I probably needed glasses. Mom took me to the local family physician. He checked my vision with a chart on the back of his office door.

"She certainly needs glasses," he said.

Another thing to make me look detestable.

My first pair cost twenty dollars. It must have taken my mom a long time to pay for them at a dollar or two a week.

I can remember seeing the blackboard at school clearly for the first time. Holy Cow! What a difference that made!

One evening, soon after I had my new glasses, my dad drove me to town for a school roller skating party. I couldn't believe how the street lights looked—tiny dots instead of large diffused blotches of light.

"Them streetlights sure look tiny with these glasses on," I said.

"Well, you take care of them things. I ain't got no money to buy another pair for you," he said.

≈

My dad did have a softer side on occasion. If he was in a good mood, he played games with us on Sunday afternoon.

"Who wants to learn how to play checkers?"

"I do," I said.

He set up the board and put the red checkers on one end and the black ones on the other. He showed me how I could hop over his and remove it from the board. If one of mine ever reached the other end of the board, he gave me a second one to set on top to make it a "king." Then I could chase him backwards and forwards until one of us had eliminated the other's pieces. He usually wiped me off the board long before I had a chance to retaliate.

I carefully watched what he did and tried to learn his strategy.

Finally, I won a game and grinned. "I beat you!" I felt quite smug about that.

He chuckled. Next time he would win again.

≈

Dad came from a family that didn't allow girls to cut their hair short, and he imposed that on my sister and me.

I questioned that rule, which seemed a bit crazy to me. "Where does it say that in the Bible?" I asked.

He looked for days until he found 1 Corinthians 11:13-15: "Is it proper for a woman to pray to God with her head uncovered? Does not even nature itself teach you that if a man has long hair, it is a dishonor to him? But if a woman has long hair, it is a glory to her; for her hair is given to her for a covering."

God says I shouldn't cut my hair, because I need my head covered. Couldn't I put on a hat or scarf?

As a young girl, Mom put curls in my hair, like Shirley Temple. But later, I wanted to wear it in a ponytail like my friends at school. All I needed was bangs so I would look great and fit in with the other girls.

One day, when I was in the seventh grade, I found an old pair of scissors, propped myself up by the kitchen sink in front of the tiny mirror on the medicine cabinet and tried to decide how much to cut off. I made a part about two inches back from my forehead.

Oops, that's probably too much.

I combed some of it back and parted off a smaller piece.

Perfect. But I wonder how far it's supposed to hang down above my eyes.

I took a good guess and had just started snipping when my mother suddenly appeared.

"What ya' doin' there?"

"I'm makin' bangs."

"Bangs? What do you need bangs for?"

"My friends wear their hair that way." I set the pair of scissors down and looked at Mom.

"Well, you know what your dad says about cutting your hair."

"It's my hair. Why can't I wear it the way I want to?"

"Rules are rules," she said, and left, shaking her head.

Dad's gonna kill me, but I'm big enough to wear my hair the way I want to, ain't I?

I finished cutting my bangs and pulled the rest of my hair back into a ponytail. I took one last peek in the mirror at my new look and felt quite pleased. My friends would be surprised.

I stayed out of sight as long as I could, but eventually became hungry enough to show up for supper. Dad didn't seem to notice at first. But then he said, "Hey, what'd you do to your hair? Who said you could cut it?"

"My friends at school wear bangs."

"I don't care what your friends do." He pounded the table for emphasis.

The words spilled out of my mouth before I could stop them. "What do you want me to do? Glue them back on?"

"Don't git smart with me," he said. "If I say you can't cut your hair, that's exactly what I mean. As long as you have your feet under my table, you're gonna do exactly what I say. Do you understand that?" His eyes shot darts at me.

"Yes, Daddy," I said. "I'll let them grow out again."

I wrote in my book:

> Don't cut my hair without Dad's permission,
> and don't even think of asking him to get my ears pierced.

Dad always said, "If God wanted you to wear earrings, he would have created you with holes in your ears."

≈

My parents also prohibited us from dancing. When I told my mother that our music teacher was showing us how to dance, she stormed in the next day, right in the middle of my eighth grade music class, and hollered at Mr. Keller, my teacher, "I heard you're teaching my kids to dance. Well, my kids ain't gonna dance!"

Disbelief covered the teacher's face. "Okay, Mrs. Bauman. I'll exempt them."

That incident didn't do much for my popularity with my friends, but I didn't dare ask questions.

I wrote in my book after school:

> I don't know what's wrong with dancing,
> but I ain't gonna do it no more.

≈

One day, when I was twelve, Clyde suggested I climb up in the grain silo and look at all the corn in the bin as Dad had recently filled it with this year's crop. I thought it would be interesting to see it so full. He ascended the ladder first and I followed.

After going up only a few of the metal steps on the 15 foot ladder attached to the inside wall of the silo, I started to get nervous.

"Don't be such a chicken," he said.

I took a few more steps up, almost to the top—and then looked down. I panicked. I couldn't do it. I could only see the machinery used to carry the grain to the top. If I fell, I'd be dead. I began to cry.

Clyde started to come down the ladder above me.

"Git goin'," he said, "or I'll step on you."

I cried and shook all the way down, one slow, shaky step at a time.

"Crybaby."

"I could have fallen into those gears."

A silo like the one Lizzy climbed

"Oh, don't be such a fraidy cat."

I felt shaken for hours afterwards. I never attempted to go up that ladder again. Until that day, ever since I'd gone down that slide in Kindergarten, I had climbed tall trees with great boldness, but the silo incident kindled a lifelong fear of heights in me.

⁓

Clyde's continuous and more frequent abuse also frightened me, but I had no one to talk to about it.

One morning I heard Molly groan and felt her shaking in the bed beside me. I peeked out of the covers and saw Clyde kneeling on her side of the bed. Whatever he had done to her had caused her to go into convulsions. Clyde looked startled and slinked back to his bedroom. I raced downstairs to get Dad, as he knew how to comfort Molly and ease her through an episode. I didn't tell him what I had seen that caused her to start convulsing. A horrible, sinking feeling swept over me as I realized that Clyde had begun doing the same unmentionable things to Molly that he was doing to me. I felt helpless against that "monster."

What am I going to do now? If I tell, all hell will break loose—both with my dad and Clyde. Dad will say I caused it somehow, and I knew the consequences of that. Clyde will just beat me to a pulp, or kill me. It won't get better. It might even get worse.

I couldn't even protect myself from Clyde. How could I help Molly? I decided nothing could be safely done. The abuse continued—now with two of us.

XV

The Milk Barn

WE HAD SIX MILK COWS, MOSTLY HOLSTEINS, WHICH BELONGED TO DAD'S boss. When it came time to bring them home from the pasture in late afternoon, Jimmy, fourteen, and I, twelve, would walk out to fetch them. We followed the well-worn paths, occasionally hopping over a fresh cow pie.

"Did you know it means good luck when you step in a cow pie?" I asked.

"You're kidding, ain't you?" He jumped over another one. "If that's the case, I'll have at least eighty years of good luck."

I don't know why old Bessie and her friends grazed as far from home as possible, but we eventually found them.

Jimmy waved his arms at them. "Git goin' back home, Bessie."

For good measure, Buster nipped one of them in the heels, and they turned and headed toward the barn.

Jimmy saved up a bunch of cow jokes for this time out to fetch them.

"Why should you never tell a cow a secret?"

"I have no idea."

"Because it will go in one ear and out the udder."

I threw back my head and howled with laughter. "Oh, you're killin' me."

"What do you call a cow that has given birth?"

"How am I supposed to know that?"

"De-Calfeinated."

"That's a bit lame."

We trudged along behind the cows, trying to avoid as many cow pies as possible.

"Wait, I have one more. A farmer said to his neighbor that he had to shoot one of his cows. 'Was it mad?' asked the second one. The first one replied, 'Well it wasn't too happy about it.'"

"Gee Willikers, that's a good one."

We weren't supposed to make the cows run or we'd have butter and cottage cheese, instead of milk, when they arrived. If they ever started to run, their giant udders swung back and forth, teats flying left and right.

"That looks udderly ridiculous," Jimmy said.

"Oh, you're a hoot."

We caught up with the cows and opened the gate for them.

When they arrived back at the barn, the cows knew enough to go on in and find their rightful places. Lightning stood on the far left, Bessie second, then the others. I gave them each a bit of grain in a bucket. When they stuck out their necks to eat, I closed the metal clamp around their head, so they could no longer back up.

Putting the metal hobbles on their hind legs scared me, so I let Jimmy do it. It was a bit tricky, especially if the cows weren't cooperative. Jimmy had to squat beside the cow and reach in front of both hind legs, snap the clip around one leg, and then hook it onto the other. That was supposed to keep them from putting their foot in the bucket while we milked them. It didn't always work. Sometimes we tied down their tails, too, so they wouldn't whop us in the face.

We had shiny five-gallon metal buckets to catch the milk. We balanced our behinds on a one-legged stool, held the large pail between our legs and squeezed the cow's nipples. It took a lot of skill. My dad and older brothers usually did the milking, but I took my turn a few times, too. The barn was filled with interesting smells—freshly mown hay, warm milk and the pungent odor of cow urine and "plop pies."

When the cats heard all the milking commotion, they descended on the barn like buzzards to road kill. They knew if they sat there quietly with a hungry look on their faces, someone would squeeze a stream of milk into their mouths. They sat up on their hind legs and reached out their front paws, trying to catch it. It was fun to watch them. After a good squirt, they licked their faces clean. My little kitten, Sylvester, used to be especially good at catching milk in mid-air. Jimmy's kitten Boots was too.

When we finished milking all the cows, we took off their hobbles, loosened the clamp from around their necks and let them go. They stayed in the fenced-in yard until morning, so we wouldn't have to fetch them at 4:30 the next day.

When we had filled the buckets, my dad took them to the house and ran the milk through a large cream separator. This machine was about four feet high and had a large bowl-like container at the top that held five gallons. The machine had dozens of metal disks inside it, which spun and separated the cream from the milk.

Our parents would ask one of us kids to turn the machine by hand. I found it difficult to start it, but then it went easier as it picked up steam. Once it spun fast enough, the cream came out of one spout and the skim milk out the other. Dad and Mom allowed us to drink as much milk as we wanted, which might have been the most nourishing, plentiful food we had. It probably saved our lives. The thought of drinking unpasteurized milk warm from the cow may not seem hygienic, but we did it. Delicious!

After we separated the milk from the cream, Dad poured the milk into giant ten-gallon cans and the cream into smaller ones. He carried them to a refrigerated room in the barn. That kept them cool until the creamery picked them up.

We used some of the cream to make our own butter. My mother put a quart of it in a container that looked like a manual hand mixer with beaters set inside a mason jar. The lid held the contraption in place. We took turns churning it, because it took at least a half hour. When it became more difficult to turn toward the end of the process, my mom would finish it. It always amazed me when it finally turned to a thick, almost white mass. We had fresh butter to put on our bread for a few days.

Our cows didn't have the decency to do their business outside, before they came in at milking time. Someone had to clean the manure out of the barn, so it would be clean before the next milking. It was a particularly unpleasant task. We had a flat, narrow shovel that fit the trough in the floor where the cows had pooped. Jimmy called it a "super, duper, pooper scooper."

After flinging the cow pies outside, we brought a couple of buckets of water in from the pump near the windmill and threw them on the floor. Good enough for tonight.

"I hope I never become a farmer's wife," I told Jimmy. "I want a clean job."

"Me, too. I'd like to travel—maybe be a trucker."

"Let's go and see what Mom made for supper."

"Okay. I'll bet it's fried potatoes with ketchup."

"Good guess." We ate every speck of what she made.

Most of what we ate came from my mother's garden, including a large store of potatoes that filled a bin in the cellar underneath our house. We didn't have balanced meals, except perhaps in the summer, when Mom grew corn, tomatoes, and cucumbers.

We called our favorite home-cooked food "goulash." Mom made it with elbow macaroni, bits of hamburger and tomato sauce. I also liked bread pudding with syrup poured over it. My mother's canned creamed corn bordered on inedible. I'm sure the pigs would have loved it.

We drank all the milk we wanted, especially after all the calves were born in the spring. If the cows dried up, we drank Pet condensed milk. To stretch it, my mom diluted it more than she was supposed to. It tasted like water, but we choked it down.

We raised our own chickens, and our Dad's boss allowed us to butcher one pig a year. We felt fortunate if we had meat once a week.

Living on the farm wasn't all that bad, but if I were going to have a better life someday, I needed to learn how to do other kinds of jobs. Some extra money to buy the things I wanted would be good, too. I decided to ask some of my friends at school where to find work.

XVI

Summers in Nebraska

Since my parents couldn't afford to buy my clothes, shoes and school supplies, I looked for a way to earn some money. I applied for a job de-tasseling corn for fifty cents an hour. Workers had to be at least twelve years old to apply, and I had reached that age the previous August. Work would last two to four weeks in July.

At the crack of dawn, I rode my bike to a designated area in town where the workers gathered. The boss picked us up in an open truck, and a dozen of us crammed into the back. The wind whipped through our hair. We waved at cars and made trucks honk as we drove along the highway. We held our noses when we passed a smelly livestock yard.

"Who farted?" one guy asked.

"He who smelt it, dealt it," another said.

One would think we were on a safari, rather than on our way to work.

When we reached the cornfield, the boss explained how the seed companies made hybrid corn and how important it was to do the job correctly. He said the farmer alternately planted two "male" rows of one kind of corn, then six "female" rows of another kind. We had to pull the tassels out of the top of every cornstalk in the female rows so the two male rows could pollinate them all. De-tasseling is not an easy job, if you imagine how high corn grows in Nebraska.

Our supervisor, an older student, assigned a row to each of us. She helped us, if we lagged behind. By the time we finished the first row, the dew on the cornstalks had soaked our clothes. I would take off my outer shirt, wring it out and put it back on to do another row.

We worked hard, but, fifty cents an hour was "big bucks" to us poor kids. Every Friday they paid us what we earned that week.

"Holy Smoke! They gave me fifteen dollars." I waved my check in the air. "I'm rich!"

By the end of the month, I had sixty to seventy dollars in my pocket. I saved most of it. I had an idea what I wanted to do someday—go to a boarding school so I wouldn't have to stay in my abusive home any longer. I could dream, right?

The following summer, when I was nearly fourteen, I found a job working in a ten-unit motel. The Jansens, members of the Congregational church we attended, owned it and the gas station next door. They paid me thirty-five cents an hour. Although I'd made more money de-tasseling corn, this job went on for the whole summer. I'd never had such wonderful cash flow over that many weeks before.

However, I didn't have the foggiest idea how to do any of the work. Mom never kept our house clean, and hadn't bothered to show me what little she did know. We didn't have indoor plumbing either, so Mrs. Jansen had to demonstrate how to clean the toilets, sinks and showers.

"Before you clean the washrooms, spray Pine-Sol on everything with this hand pump to kill the germs."

"Germs? What's that?"

Mrs. Jansen tried to explain how the people who stayed in the motel left behind microscopic organisms. We needed to kill them so we, and the next guests, wouldn't become sick.

No one had ever mentioned germs at our house. I couldn't see the darn things, but I sprayed those imaginary bugs anyway. The Pine-Sol stank and made me sneeze.

After I mastered washrooms, I helped Mrs. Jansen change sheets and mop the linoleum floors with some kind of oil. As I learned more, she put me in charge of doing the laundry after I had finished cleaning all the rooms.

"Hang these sheets on the line outside," she said. "Be careful not to drop one on the ground, or we'll have to start over."

She didn't have a system for keeping the 72 inch-wide sheets for the twin beds separate from the 81 inch-wide ones for the double beds. She spent a lot of time looking through the piles of clean ones for the right size.

The solution seemed simple to me. I organized the sheets when I hung them on the clothesline. I looked for the size on the tag on the bottom hem, and then hung all of the single sheets on one line and the double ones on the next. After they dried, I folded them like that, keeping the two sizes separate.

Mrs. Jansen showed me how to iron the sheets and pillowcases with an old-fashioned mangle. I slowly guided them through it several times until they looked smooth. Then I put the 72 inch-ones in one pile in the linen cupboard and the 81 inch-ones in a separate pile. Mrs. Jansen soon noticed what I had done.

"You're a genius," she said. "Why didn't I ever think of that?"

"I saw how you struggled to find the right size every day, so I invented a new system."

"You deserve a raise."

The next time she paid me, she gave me fifty cents an hour. I was ecstatic.

I often went to work without breakfast, so Mrs. Jansen would give me a glass of Tang and a bite to eat before I started cleaning. She often prayed with me during this time. She encouraged me every day. I loved working for her—much better than for my mom in the mess at home.

≈

Our house was located on a country road, about a quarter of a mile from the local cemetery. Dad always said, "They're our best neighbors. They never cause us no problems."

After I finished working at the motel, Jimmy and I liked to ride over on our bikes and wander through the graveyard to see how many names we recognized. We found the grave of Mr. Slovak, my sixth grade teacher's husband, and a few others we knew. We liked reading the epitaphs and noticing how old the people were when they died.

"One should say, 'I told you I was sick,'" Jimmy said.

"You're funny."

We rode around for a bit and stopped to check out another row of headstones.

"Do you know why they put fences around cemeteries?" he asked.

"No, why?"

"Because people are dying to git in here."

"Ha! Or, maybe, it's to keep them in after they're here."

We rode along through a few more rows of graves and stopped by one with a large headstone.

"I heard about some kids playing in the cemetery one evening," Jimmy said. "They heard a tap, tap, tapping sound. It frightened them, but they went closer to see what made the noise."

"What was it?"

"When they peeked around a headstone a few feet away, they saw a guy with a small hammer and a chisel."

"What was he doin' with that?"

"They tip-toed even closer. He seemed harmless, so they got brave enough to go over and ask him. 'What ya' doin' there?' He said, 'They misspelled my name. I'm fixin' it.' That's when they ran home in a hurry."

"Great Caesar's Ghost!" I said. "We'd better git out of here. You're scaring me."

Jimmy burst out laughing.

Cemeteries and dead people weren't the only things that scared me. Dad and Clyde did, too. I often sat in the rocking chair with my knees under my chin and my arms wrapped around my legs. I rocked for hours. It provided a bit of comfort for my troubled soul. The nights scared me the most. I never knew when Clyde would show up beside my bed. I often woke up screaming. No one came to find out why. I found it difficult to go back to sleep after that.

≈

It didn't matter how little sleep I got, I had to work at the motel again the next day. Mrs. Jansen was also the custodian of our small church. One day, just as I was about to go to the laundry room, I heard her talking to Pastor Rever on the telephone.

"Hello, Pastor. What's up? . . . You're having a funeral there this afternoon? . . . No, I haven't had time to clean since the last service. I'll ask Lizzy to help me. She's cleaning the motel this morning. . . . Okay, we'll get right on it. Bye."

I agreed to help, because I thought we would finish before the hearse came. I was terrified of dead people. I couldn't even look at a photo of a person in a coffin. It gave me the heebie-jeebies.

As I vacuumed the sanctuary, which seated about seventy-five people, the funeral home director and his assistant rolled the casket down the center aisle and maneuvered it into place at the front of our church. No!

I ran over to where Mrs. Jansen was cleaning a classroom.

"They brought the casket in!" I whispered.

"I told you we needed to clean for a funeral." She continued dusting.

"But I didn't want to be here when they came."

"He's dead. He isn't going to hurt you. Now go back and finish cleaning."

My hands shook as I worked. I straightened the hymnbooks and dusted the pews, keeping a wary eye on the casket the whole time.

Don't open that lid!

The funeral director and his helper brought in several bouquets of flowers and set them on either side of the casket.

"Lots of flowers. He must have been a well-liked man."

"Looks that way," the other one said.

I hooked up the vacuum and started cleaning the choir loft and the area behind the pulpit. I tried to hurry, but still do a good job.

After the funeral director had arranged all the flowers, he opened the casket—right in front of me. Great Caesar's Ghost! I gasped. My knees turned to jelly. I started to shake all over. I tried not to look, but I quickly glanced to see if the body stirred. I feared he would sit up, jump out and chase me down the aisle. Maybe it was all those scary cemetery stories Jimmy had told me. Anyway, no one has ever cleaned as fast as I did those last few minutes.

I fled out of the church as soon as we finished. It took a long time to pull myself back together. I hoped I wouldn't have to go to a funeral for a long time.

≈

By the fifth summer of working for the Jansens, they would go away to Iowa to visit relatives for the weekend and leave me in charge. I checked in the guests and cleaned up after them the next day. Sometimes I also worked for Mr. Jansen at the gas station.

An old farmer I knew drove up one day. "Fill up the oil and check the gas?" I asked.

He grinned. "It don't burn oil that bad."

"I'm joking." I removed the gas cap and started filling the tank.

"Hey, why's a young girl like you working in a gas station?"

"I'm saving money to go to school." I washed his windshield and dried it with a squeegee.

"Ain't that boys' work?"

"Work is work. If they can do it, so can I." I finished filling the tank. "That will be seven dollars and fifty-nine cents, please."

I enjoyed all the jobs I did and learned to do them well. My bank account continued to increase.

Someday I'll go out on my own. I'll find a safe place to live and take care of myself. But first I have to finish school. Better keep working.

XVII

Getting Into More Trouble

WHENEVER I DIDN'T HAVE TO WORK, I SPENT TIME WITH JIMMY. Sometimes he and I played tricks on each other. He would go outside, knock on the front door and then laugh when I opened it, because I'd expected a visitor, not him.

I quickly caught on to his little prank. The next time I heard a knock on the door, I whipped it open, bowed, and said, "Come in, dear sir." When I looked up, there stood my mother's elderly lady friend from church. I slammed the door, raced upstairs and waited for the embarrassment to drain out of my body. I felt so rotten. I added another black spot to my heart that day.

My mother later said she had apologized to Mrs. Tessman and explained what Jimmy and I had been doing. My rude actions hadn't impressed either of them, but at least Mom understood.

I had a difficult time greeting this lady at church the next Sunday. I looked down at the floor when I saw her coming.

"That wasn't a nice thing to do, was it Lizzy?"

"No, I'm sorry. I won't do that again."

She put her arm around my shoulder and said, "It's okay. I forgive you. I figured you were playing."

"Thanks, Mrs. Tessman."

She forgives me? I wish my parents would forgive me for all the bad things I've done. Maybe punishment is their way of doing that. It felt good to be forgiven by Mrs. Tessman.

≈

We didn't always have enough to eat. To remedy our hunger problem, Jimmy and I sneaked into the pantry and made a treat by mixing a glob of Crisco shortening and white sugar. We mushed it into a ball, raced outside and ate it. We must have made a mess doing it, because one day Mom caught us.

"Who's been taking my ingredients from the pantry?"

If I admit it, I'll get whipped. If I lie, she probably won't believe me, and then I'll get punished for lying. I'd better tell the truth, like Mrs. Petracek taught us in Sunday school.

"Jimmy and I done it."

"It ain't good for you to eat that much grease."

"But we were hungry."

She started peeling some potatoes for our next meal. "Next time, eat a piece of bread with jam on it,"

"That's all we ever git to eat."

"I'm fryin' up spuds for dinner."

I knew it was useless to protest any further.

≈

When Jimmy turned fourteen, he bought himself a pellet gun with money he earned picking up corn off the ground for a farmer the fall before. We practiced shooting tin cans off a fence post. I could shoot more accurately than he could, but that didn't offend him. One day as we sat behind the house, a flock of Mom's chickens meandered by and Jimmy took aim.

"You're not gonna kill a chicken, are you?"

"Naw, I can't hit the broad side of a barn."

He took aim. "POP!"

One of mom's laying hens fell over and started twitching.

"Now, don't that beat all? I hit it."

"You killed a chicken. Now Mom's gonna kill you."

"What should we do with it?"

"I don't know. We're in *big* trouble."

We ran over to the chicken and watched it twitch its last. Jimmy took off his hat, placed it reverently across his heart and bowed his head for a moment. "Thank you, Hennie, for all those eggs you laid for us." He donned his hat again.

"Maybe we should quick dig a hole and bury it."

"She'll miss it though. She knows how many she has."

"Maybe we could say it got hit by a car on the road."

"That's a good idea."

He picked up the lifeless hen and took it to the house, dangling it by its feet, to show to Mom.

"Now what'd you go and do with that chicken?"

"Nothin'," he said. "Mr. Anderson whizzed by in his red pickup and 'Bam!' He banged right into it."

"You know we ain't got many hens left to lay eggs."

"I'm sorry Mom. Maybe we could fry it for dinner and it won't be wasted."

"I s'pose so."

She took the dead hen over to the woodpile and chopped off its head. Then she boiled some water and dipped the chicken in it to loosen the feathers before she proceeded to clean it. Jimmy and I sneaked the dismembered head behind the chicken barn and checked it. It was a bit bloody, but Jimmy examined it carefully until he felt something hard. Sure enough, the pellet had struck it right behind the eye.

I nearly barfed. "Poor Hennie."

"I'm a purdy good shot," he said.

"Yeah, but maybe you should stick to shooting tin cans from now on."

The fried hen for dinner tasted a bit tough, but we ate it heartily. Jimmy and I exchanged mischievous glances. While thinking about how our dinner had died, I hoped Jimmy and I could keep a fit of the giggles away.

As we ate, I leaned over and whispered in his ear, "You're such a good brother."

"Well, you ain't such a bad sister neither," he whispered back.

"What're you two whispering about?" Mom asked. "You'd better not be hatchin' no more trouble."

"We ain't," Jimmy said.

As he finished his chicken and turned away from me, for one quick second I wondered if maybe I could tell him about Clyde and the awful secret I'd never been able to share. I slowly bit off a piece of my chicken leg and pondered that option.

If I tell him, what if he confronts Clyde? He'll probably beat up both of us. He said he would kill me if I ever told. He might even kill both of us.

I took another bite and glanced at my mother. She picked up her plate and took it to the sink. She came back with a washcloth to wipe Molly's dirty face and hands. "When you're finished eatin', you need to worsh up these dishes."

It would be worse if Jimmy tells Mom. She won't believe it or do anything about it. She lets Clyde git by with murder around here.

I wiped my greasy mouth on my sleeve and glanced at my father, who sat reading the Columbus Telegram. He scowled at me still sitting there. "What ya' waitin' for? Your mom needs help with the dishes."

Telling Dad will git us all strapped. That's the last thing I want.

I swallowed my last bite of chicken, but it didn't want to go down. My stomach lurched, and I almost spit it up. I quickly took a sip of milk, as my eyes locked with Jimmy's.

I'd better not tell. I'm in enough trouble around here as it is.

≈

In early December of 1958, Grandma called our house with a surprising invitation.

Mom handed the phone to me. "Hi, Lizzy," Grandma said. "How would you and Jimmy like to take the bus up and visit us for Christmas?"

"Wow! Are you kidding?"

"No, I'm serious. We'll send your parents the money to buy the tickets. And we'll pick you up at the bus depot in Longville."

"Thanks, Grandma! I'll start packin'. Bye! I love you!"

I hung up the phone, found Jimmy and broke the news to him.

"We're goin' to Grandpa and Grandma's for Christmas!"

"Who said?"

"Grandma called. She's sendin' us money to buy the tickets."

"Now, don't that beat all? I didn't think we'd ever go there."

I was fourteen. Jimmy had turned sixteen at the end of November and had taken up smoking.

"Grandma ain't gonna like seein' you smoke," I said. "You'd better quit before we go."

He quit that day and never smoked again.

We had never been out of Nebraska, so the thought of being that far from home scared me a bit. What frightened me even more was the thought of my sweet Molly being left at home alone with Clyde across the hall from her bedroom. I prayed that God would protect her.

We kept our eyes glued to the window of the bus as we travelled and pointed out the new sights to each other. By the end of the 15-hour trip, we were dog-tired.

Grandpa and Grandma hugged the life out of us when we descended from the bus. Then they drove us in their car along a winding road through the woods to their small cabin.

We played on the frozen lake and made giant messages for our grandparents by dragging our boots in the snow. "Merry Christmas, Grandpa and Grandma! We love you." That delighted them. Grandpa smiled and waved from the cabin window. Grandma clapped her hands.

We didn't have skates, but we shoveled the snow aside for a place to slide around on our boots. I worried about falling through the ice, until I saw several cars driving on the lake. "That ice is two feet thick," Grandpa said.

Nebraska winters are cold, but Minnesota's are worse. Some nights the temperature dropped to minus 35°Fahrenheit (minus 37°Celsius). The snow made a loud crunching sound when we walked on it. When it warmed up a bit during the day, they took us for walks through the woods. The scenery amazed us—millions of birch trees, deer running in the woods, birds we had never seen before.

We watched Grandpa cut a hole in the ice to fetch buckets of water for use in the house. It amused us to see them flush the toilet with a pail of water. Of course, our house didn't even have a toilet, so we couldn't really laugh.

They didn't buy many gifts for us for Christmas. We weren't used to getting much anyway, so that didn't matter. The trip far exceeded anything we could have dreamed of.

Grandpa and Grandma's house in Minnesota

After two weeks of playing Monopoly and card games with Grandpa and Grandma, we had to return home. Jimmy and I chatted unceasingly about our new experiences all the way, and the memories brought us both joy for years.

XVIII

A Wild Ride

AFTER WORK, I COULD DO WHATEVER I LIKED—PLAY WITH MOLLY, RIDE bicycles with Jimmy or sit in the rocking chair and read. We also had a couple of workhorses on our farm, and I often rode Charlie out to the pasture. Before riding, I gave him some corn to eat—bribery, I suppose. Dad taught me how to come up behind the horses without startling them.

"You have to say something to them and pat them on the behind so they know you're coming," he said. "Otherwise they might kick your teeth out."

I didn't want that to happen, so I let them know when I arrived at the barn to feed and groom them.

"Hey, Charlie, want some grain?" I patted him on the nose. I figured the front end of the horse was safer than the back.

By the time I turned 13, I could put a bridle in Charlie's mouth by myself, hop on from the feed trough or the gate outside the barn, and go trotting off to the pasture. I rode bareback, as we couldn't afford a saddle.

I could never make him gallop, though, as he was a farm horse, not a thoroughbred. I preferred hightailing it across the pasture at top speed, but he never cooperated. Clyde and Jimmy couldn't make him go as well as I did. Charlie would go to about the middle of the pasture for them, turn around and head for home.

One day, after watching them, I bragged. "Watch me. I can make him go past the middle."

I hopped on and trotted out to the pasture. When we reached the middle, he turned around abruptly, sending me airborne. I brushed myself off, caught up to him, and grabbed the reins. I couldn't mount him again without a fence to climb. I returned a bit more humble.

~

Another time, when I was fourteen, I decided to take Charlie across Highway 30, over the railroad tracks and down a country road past our mailbox. All went well for a short while. He obeyed my "giddy up" and "whoa" signals. Then, about two miles from home, I suddenly heard shots. "BANG! BANG!"

Oh, no! It's hunting season. Someone must have shot at something in the woods.

Charlie took off for home "like a shot out of a gun," (pardon the pun) with me hanging on for dear life.

"Whoa! Whoa!" I hollered.

He galloped down the back road.

As we neared the railroad tracks, I gripped the reins tighter with my right hand and a hunk of mane with my left. I looked left and right, terrified that I might see a train. "Whoa, Charlie!" I yelled.

He didn't listen.

"Whoa!" I shrieked. "Look out for trucks!"

He raced across the highway, and it's a miracle I'm alive to tell this tale. When we reached our farm, I'm not sure who sweated the most, the horse or me.

Jimmy saw me coming back.

"That's the wildest ride I've ever had." I slid off as soon as Charlie finally came to a halt on our driveway. "I didn't know he could go that fast."

"I'm surprised you didn't fall off," Jimmy said.

My legs were still shaking as I took Charlie back to the barn, gave him a treat and groomed him.

When I finished, I patted him on the nose. "Thanks for the ride, Charlie. I like to go fast like that, but you have to learn to look out for trains and trucks."

≈

Jimmy waited for me. "Let's go play out by the water tank. But first, let's git my hat from the porch." His hat hung on the same nail as the dreaded strap. Seeing the strap made me shudder and I turned away quickly and skipped off with Jimmy.

Our pasture bordered on Highway 30. An old windmill for pumping water into a steel tank for the horses and cattle stood close to the wooden fence at the side of the highway. The water tank had a lot of dark green, slimy moss growing inside it. Jimmy thought it would be fun to lob a gob of the gooey stuff over the fence and onto the highway and then quickly duck down before anyone saw where it came from.

We both had fun pitching handfuls, until Jimmy flung one that flew right through the open window of a pickup truck and hit the driver. He slammed on the brakes and looked around.

Jimmy and I fled to the house. From the upstairs bedroom window, we could see the man talking to our dad out in the field.

When Dad came home for dinner, he said, "Some guy claimed one of my kids threw a hunk of moss in his truck window. Does anyone know anything about that?"

We tried to look innocent. We both stared at the floor, our hands covering our behinds.

"I told him my kids would never do a foolish thing like that."

We started to breathe a bit easier.

"But, to be sure, I'm going out to see if there's any evidence."

While Dad went to the water tank, Jimmy took the strap off the hook in the back porch and hid it in the woodpile.

"He's gonna be even madder when he finds that missing."

"Maybe, he'll cool off while he's looking for it."

"How likely is that?"

"Not likely. You're right. It probably wasn't a good idea."

We waited for the inevitable. Dad thundered back into the house. "There's dozens of gobs of moss on the highway. Who did that?"

"Lizzy and I did. We're sorry. We won't do it again."

Hiding the strap was *not* a good idea. Dad found another belt and whipped our backsides until we were sore. We never threw moss bombs again. We would have to find a new way to entertain ourselves. Besides, summer was almost over. It would be time to go back to school soon—Jimmy to the twelfth grade and I to the tenth.

XIX

Hope

BY THE TIME I REACHED FOURTEEN, I SECRETLY HOPED FOR SOME WAY TO escape from my home. If only I had somewhere to go and someone to help me. If I could ever find a way out, I'd pounce on it.

I spent a lot of time at the home of the Revers, my pastor and his wife. I felt safe with them. I helped her clean house, and I often sat quietly in a corner of his office and read a book, while he worked on his next sermon.

One afternoon, he swiveled his chair around to face me. "Is something bothering you, Lizzy?"

There are a lot of things bothering me, but I can't talk about them.

"No, but I feel better at your house."

"If you want to talk, I'm here to listen. I'll finish this sermon later." He closed his notebook.

"Do you remember when you gave everyone a Bible reading schedule on New Year's Day?"

"Yes, are you using it?"

"Yeah, I started in Genesis last January, and I'm halfway through the whole Bible already."

He took off his glasses and laid them on his desk. "That's great!" He chuckled. "I'm glad someone listens to my suggestions. I hope you're learning a lot from the Good Book."

"Yeah, there's some great stories in there."

I wished I could tell Pastor Rever about the verse I found in Leviticus 18:9, which says, "Do not have sexual relations with your sister." I was horrified when I read that. My brother Clyde had been doing that to me since I was seven. I decided right then that I was going to put a stop to it.

I pondered what I had learned from the text in Leviticus. The next time Clyde knelt beside my bed, reached under the covers and started to touch me, I kicked him in the face. "No! I ain't doin' this no more!"

"What do you mean?" he asked.

"I don't want you to touch me again—ever!"

To my surprise, he stopped and stood up. He looked down at me. "What am I going to do now?" He looked pathetic.

"Find someone else," I shouted. "Get married. But leave me and my sister alone."

He narrowed his eyes and returned to his room, picked up a large Webster's dictionary, came back and threw it hard at me. It missed me but hit my little sister Molly in the head. She woke up screaming. Then he came back a second time, far angrier, and started methodically lifting the end of my bed up and crashing it against the floor until the crossbars broke.

My parents came running upstairs. "What the Sam Hill is going on here?" Dad shouted.

She had her light on, and I couldn't git to sleep," Clyde said.

"Is that true, Lizzy?" Dad asked.

Of course it wasn't, but I didn't want to receive a beating for telling the truth. "Yes. I was reading my Bible, but this bulb is so dim, it shouldn't bother him none."

"Well, git that light off at bedtime. You can read some other time," Dad said. "If I hear any more noise up here, someone is gonna git strapped."

I wanted so badly to tell Pastor Rever all that, but I couldn't. "I'd better let you get back to your sermon. I'll go help Mrs. Rever."

I went to the kitchen and helped her dry the dinner dishes.

"You spend a lot of time here," she said. "Is everything okay at home?"

"Not really."

"I've noticed things seem a bit tense in your family."

Tense? Holy Cow! Is it ever tense!

I grabbed a dish she had washed and wiped it a lot longer than necessary.

"Yeah, Dad blows up every so often and beats the heck out of me."

"You're fourteen. Aren't you a bit old to be spanked?"

"Tell *him* that."

I set a stack of clean dishes in the cupboard.

"I wish there was a Christian high school around here for you to attend," she said. "The closest one is in Kansas."

"That's too far away, and me and my parents ain't got no money for that anyway."

"We can't afford to help you either. My husband and I will pray for your safety, though, and for a miracle."

"Thanks, Mrs. Rever."

My mom probably had a lot of work for me to do too. I hung up my wet towel, gave Mrs. Rever a hug and left for home.

≈

For a whole year after that conversation, I mulled over the idea of escaping to a boarding school. It seemed hopeless that I would ever break free. I felt like I was in prison and wrote a poem about it in my little book:

Prison Child

My home is like a prison, its horror very real.
It's difficult to tell you how I really feel.

The meals are often sparse; who cares if I get fed?
At night the many mice play games beneath my bed.

The captain of the prison will often rage and roar.
The beatings that he gives me leave me bruised and sore.

Hope

My prison guard is worse; how can he molest a child?
Does he know what shame and guilt upon my heart he's piled?

I huddle in a corner, shivering in the cold,
Wondering how to escape, trying to be bold.

How will you believe me when I tell you such a tale?
Well, let me now assure you that it is very, very real.

The jail is just my home; the captain is my father.
The cell is my small room; the guard my oldest brother.

I'm just a little child; I pray, "God, help me, please!"
My heart is filled with terror; will this nightmare never cease?

Will God look down in mercy and see me in my cell?
Will he rescue my poor soul from this awful living hell?

Lizzy Bauman 1959

A week before I would be starting the tenth grade at Clarks Public School, I arrived at church on Sunday morning and looked for Pastor and Mrs. Rever. I didn't see either of them so I checked the bulletin. It said: Our pastor is away for a conference this weekend, so we have invited Mr. Kevin Spencer from Nebraska Christian High School in Central City to lead the service. He is the head of the music department.

A Christian high school in Central City? Only thirteen miles from here? When did that open?

I listened intently to the sermon that morning. Mr. Spencer, a friendly young man in his early-twenties, preached about Joseph, whose brothers abused him and sold him into slavery in Egypt. He reminded us that Joseph never gave up hope, even during the time he spent in prison. Eventually, he became free and helped many people.

113

Near the end of the service, Mr. Spencer told us about the new Christian high school opening the last week of August—only a week away. He encouraged anyone of high school age to talk to him after the service.

My ears perked up. Did I dare hope? I wanted to hear more about it, so I ran up to him after the service.

"I want to know more about the new school."

"What's your name, young lady?"

"Elizabeth Bauman, but everyone calls me Lizzy." I looked around to see if my parents noticed me talking to him.

"What grade will you be in?"

"I'll be a sophomore."

"You have three years of high school left. Are you interested in going?"

Am I interested in going? I've waited my whole life for this opportunity.

"Yeah, but . . . but how much does it cost to go there?"

"About five hundred dollars a year would cover your tuition, room and board."

Holy Toledo!

My face fell. I stared at the floor, thinking of the trifling amount of money I had in the bank.

"Do you have some way to pay for that?" he asked.

I turned away for a minute and rubbed the back of my neck. When I finally had the courage to look up again, I barely whispered. "I have ninety dollars saved from working at the motel."

"That's a good start. Can your parents help you?"

I looked down again. "No, they ain't got much money. They could never help me."

"How have you done in your studies?"

I looked up and smiled. "I was on the honor roll every semester in the ninth grade. And I won a medal in a math contest."

"It sounds like you're a good student. Why don't you fill out an application? Some of the students can do jobs around the school to help work off their debt."

My eyebrows shot up. "I know how to work real hard. I've had a job since I was twelve. I'll do anything you want me to."

He gave me a four-page application. I folded it in half and tucked it into my Bible.

I have an application. I can't believe it's even a possibility.

"Thanks, Mr. Spencer."

"You're welcome. I hope we hear from you."

Oh, you'll hear from me.

I spun around and raced out the door to catch a ride home with my family.

⁓

After dinner, I went up to my bedroom and, with the stub of an old pencil, started to fill out my application to Nebraska Christian High School.

I can't believe there's a private school this close to my home. And I have an application to go there. Is this the miracle Mrs. Rever talked about? Of course, filling this out doesn't git me there. What if they don't accept me with no means to pay? What if my parents won't let me go? Oh, God, I need a miracle. Please. Please.

Jimmy found me in my room and asked, "What ya' doin'?"

"You remember that man who preached at our church this morning?"

"Yeah."

"He gave me an application to go to that new high school in Central City. I'm fillin' it out and I'm gonna mail it tomorrow."

Jimmy frowned. "Do you think Dad will let you go? Mom's pregnant, you know."

He's right. Dad won't let me leave. Mom will need my help.

"I don't know, but Mom might." I had a smidgen of hope in my heart.

"Well, good luck with that. If you ever need a ride up to the school, I'll take you in my old Ford."

As he headed for his own room, I smiled. "Thanks. You're a good brother."

≈

On Monday morning, I found an envelope and a stamp for my application. I jumped on my bike and hurried to the mailbox mounted on a rotting post on the other side of the highway and railroad tracks, set the letter inside it and raised the red flag.

Dear God, this is Lizzy. I'm here to ask a favor of you. Please let me be accepted by Nebraska Christian. I'd like to live somewhere safe. Could you at least let my mom be in favor of me goin' there? Thanks.

I knew I wouldn't receive an answer from the school on Tuesday—too early. On Wednesday, I biked to the mailbox to see if they had responded. Nope, not yet. Doubts crowded into my heart.

How could I even think of going to that school? They probably won't want me, if I can't pay my tuition. Mom might let me go, but Dad? How on earth will I ever git past him?

On Thursday, I biked to the mailbox a half hour before the mailman arrived.

"Any letters for the Baumans?" I asked.

"Three today."

"Any for me—Lizzy?"

"Let's see," he said. "Yep, from Nebraska Christian High School." He shook his head. "Never heard of it."

"I have." I grabbed it out of his hand.

As he drove off, I prayed. *Please, God. Please.*

My heart pounded in my chest as I carefully opened the white envelope. I held my breath and slowly unfolded the single sheet of paper. It had the name of the school written in bold letters across the top. "Dear Lizzy, We are happy to inform you that your application to Nebraska Christian High School has been accepted. School starts next Monday. We look forward to meeting you." Mr. Everheart, the superintendent, had signed it.

I screamed. I waved the letter in the air. I cried. I jumped on my bike and started for home as fast as I could, so excited I forgot to look for a train at the railroad crossing. I slammed on my brakes when I heard the shrill whistle and saw the bright headlight coming at me.

I backed up and counted the cars on the freight train—ninety-five, ninety-six, ninety-seven. As the caboose went by, I looked and saw another one coming from the other direction.

Oh, Criminy! Now I have to wait for another slowpoke. Who am I gonna show this letter to first? Jimmy? Mrs. Rever? Mom? Not Dad, that's for sure.

I counted again. Eighty-five, eighty-six, eighty-seven. Finally, I crossed the tracks and waited briefly by the highway for a semi-truck to go by. Our house was about a quarter of a mile away. I pedaled like crazy and dropped my bike on our gravel driveway. I could hardly breathe.

Okay, git a grip. Think about how you're gonna break the news to Mom. She's expecting a baby. Take it easy on her.

I took the letter to my room, plunked down on my bed and read it over and over.

They accepted me! They really accepted me! Thank you, God. It's a miracle!

When I came back downstairs, Mom was kneading a batch of bread. "Any mail today?"

"There's a telephone bill, a letter from Grandma and one for me from Nebraska Christian High School."

"Oh? What'd they send you a letter for?"

She walked over to me with her hands covered with sticky bread dough. I hid the letter behind my back.

"Mr. Spencer, the man who preached on Sunday gave me an application."

"You sent it in," her voice rose, "and didn't even discuss it with us?"

I backed up a pace, straightened my back and clasped my arms together tightly.

"I really want to go there. They accepted my application and I can start on Monday."

"What do you mean? We don't have no money to send you to a private school. How much does it cost to go there?"

"Five hundred dollars," I squeaked.

"Five hundred dollars?" She gasped and clasped her hand over her mouth. Flour and dough clung to her face. "Where are you gonna git that much money?"

Uh-oh. This is worse than I expected. If I can't git past Mom, what will it be like to tell Dad?

"I have ninety dollars saved in the bank. They said I could set tables, wash dishes and help in the kitchen after school to pay the rest."

"Who told you that?"

"Mr. Spencer."

I pulled the letter out from behind my back and gave it to her. She read it, then pinched her nose, adding more flour to her face. She read it again.

Please, God. Let her say yes.

Finally, she said, "We can't help you. But if you pay for everything yourself, you have my permission to go."

Did she give me her permission? I can't believe it.

"Thanks, Mom."

"But you have to tell Dad when he comes home from work. He ain't gonna like what you've done."

I took my letter back and brushed the flour off it. Then I ran outside and found Jimmy fixing a flat tire on his car.

"Guess what? The school accepted my application."

"Hey, that's great! Did you tell Mom?"

I grinned at him. "She said I could go."

"Well, I'll be darned. I didn't think she'd let you." He tightened the nuts on the wheel.

"Me neither."

Jimmy picked up his tools and put them back in the toolbox. We hopped on our bikes and sped off down the gravel road.

I clutched the handlebars tightly. "How will I ever git permission from Dad?"

"I don't know. He thinks girls don't need no education. He says they git married and have babies. All that money would be wasted."

"Wasted?" I frowned. "Wouldn't it make me a better mother to be educated?"

"I s'pose so," he said. We turned the corner and headed down another road.

"Anyway," I said, "I ain't gittin' married 'til I'm at least twenty-one. After I finish high school, I'm goin' to college and study to be a teacher."

"You'll make a mighty fine one, too. I seen you helpin' Molly with her schoolwork."

"Thanks, Jimmy. You're my best friend."

We returned home at suppertime.

Now I have to break the news to Dad. Lord, have mercy. He expects me to help Mom with the housework—washin' the clothes and scrubbin' the floors. And she's pregnant again. Good grief! Ain't it about time she quits havin' babies? Clyde's almost twenty.

"Set the table for me, okay?" Mom said.

I grabbed a pile of our mismatched, chipped plates and looked at the stove. Mom hadn't burned anything tonight, so maybe Dad would be in a good mood. After everyone said grace, we dug in. I glanced at Mom; she had a worried look on her face.

I took a bite of fried potatoes covered with ketchup, but the food stuck in my throat. I washed it down with some milk.

I stole furtive glances at Dad as he ate.

When he had finished and started sipping his cup of coffee, I finally screwed up my courage, cleared my throat, and said, "Dad, you remember that visiting minister we had on Sunday, who told us about the new Christian high school in Central City?"

"Yeah," he said. "What about it?"

"I'd like to go there."

"Over my dead body."

My muscles tensed. "Why can't I go?"

"Your mom needs you around here. She's gonna have another baby in a few months. Why in tarnation would you want to go there?"

"It would be a good place to learn. All the kids and teachers are Christians." I hoped that would persuade him.

"You have a good high school right here in Clarks—and it's free."

Okay, tell him the truth.

"I sent in my application on Monday," I said slowly. I wrapped my arms around myself to prepare for the inevitable blow. "They sent me a letter of acceptance today."

"What the Sam Hill is goin' on here?" He shook his fist at me. "Who gave you permission to do that?"

"Mom did."

I saw the look of terror in her eyes as his face turned red and he started yelling.

"Why'd you do that, Woman?"

Mom hung her head and wrung her hands in her lap. "She really wants to go, and she does so well in school."

"Who's paying for this?" He clenched his fists. "It ain't comin' out of my wages."

I took a shaky breath. "I have some money saved in the bank. The school said I could work off the rest."

"Your mother needs you here at home."

"Mom says I can do my chores when I come home for the week-end."

"You've got an answer for everything, don't you?" He slammed his fist on the table and stared at Mom. "Well, dad-blasted! Why don't no one listen to what I think?" He jumped up from the table.

I started to shake. *Is he going for the strap?*

He glared at me. "Someday," he said, "when you stand over your mother's grave, you'll be sorry you left."

He turned and stomped out of the house.

I took one look at Mom and knew something had changed. The war wasn't over, but I had won *this* battle. Completely drained, I left quietly, went up to my bedroom and crawled under the covers, even though it wasn't bedtime.

Sometimes God does answer my prayers.

Dear God, It's me . . . Lizzy again. Thank you that Mom gave me permission to go to Nebraska Christian. Dad is mad as hell. Help me not to git beaten again before I leave. I'll do anything to pay you back. I'll be a missionary, or whatever you want.

Hope

The next morning, I found an old cardboard box and started packing my clothes. School started in three days.

XX

Beginning a New Life

On Friday, after I received my acceptance letter, Mom took Molly and me shopping in Central City to buy sheets, a blanket and a bedspread for my bunk bed at the dorm. Mom paid five dollars of the bill, and I paid the rest.

"Are you going away?" Molly asked.

"Only during the week. I'll come home on Saturday and Sunday."

"I'm gonna miss you."

"I'm gonna miss you, too." I squeezed her hand.

While at Ben Franklin's Five and Dime, I noticed some sewing material. "Can you make me a pair of pajamas before I go, Mom? I'd be embarrassed to sleep in my dress."

"We'll have to hurry. What color of material do you want?"

I searched through the stacks. Finally, I saw a red and white candy stripe that tickled my fancy. "This one."

"I'll need a pattern, too."

I picked a two-piece set with a long-sleeved top. The clerk cut off a few yards of material and added up what I owed. I paid for it out of my wages from working at the motel.

Mom sewed for hours on Saturday. I had taken sewing in Home Economics class in the ninth grade, so I helped sew around the buttonholes by hand and attached the buttons for her. "I'm going to have the best pajamas in the whole school."

Mom looked pleased.

"I wish I had some like that," Molly said.

"I have a bit of material left. Would you like me to make a blanket for your dolly?"

"Yeah!" She hopped up and down and gave me a hug.

After I finished sewing it, I gave it to her.

"When I miss you, I'll hug my blankie." She held it close to her face. Her chocolate eyes sparkled.

I hugged her until she squeaked.

≈

On Monday, August 24, 1959—the pivotal day of my life—I started a new life.

Thank you, God. Thank you!

Mom dropped me off at the school. I set my two boxes near the entrance and went to the business office to register.

Mr. Everheart, the superintendent greeted me. "Welcome to Nebraska Christian." He smiled and shook my hand.

Nebraska Christian High School, as it appeared in 2012

"Thanks for accepting my application on such short notice," I said.

"Glad to have you. Let's go over to Mr. Baker, the business administrator. You can pay your fees to him."

I took a deep breath and fingered the ninety dollars I had in my dress pocket.

We discussed my account, and I handed my life savings to him. I felt drained—like my bank account.

"Mr. Everheart said your parents won't be helping you, so we've lined up a few jobs. We pay our students fifty cents an hour," Mr. Baker said.

"Thank you. I'll be happy to do whatever you want."

After I registered for my classes with Miss Wilson, the secretary, I left for the dorm, where I met Mr. and Mrs. Spencer, who supervised the girls.

"I'm glad you made it, Lizzy. You had a lot of doubts when I talked to you a few days ago," Mr. Spencer said.

"No kidding! I'm still pinching myself to see if this is really happening."

"We're happy to have you." Mrs. Spencer's smile warmed me. "Let me show you to your room."

I soon met my roommate, a sophisticated and worldly-wise senior. She and I, a country bumpkin sophomore, had a difficult time adjusting to one another. I had spent most of my life in fear and dread. Living with someone I didn't know engendered new fears.

"Bottom bunk or top?" she asked.

"Bottom. I'm afraid I might fall out," I said. "My sister broke her collar bone falling out of a regular bed."

We had a small closet. Her clothes took up at least three quarters of it. It was a good thing I didn't have much to hang up. It terrified me to dress and undress with her around. If I couldn't do it in the dark after turning off the light, I squeezed inside the closet and dressed there. No wonder she thought I was crazy.

I was as quiet as a mouse; she was loud. I liked things neat and clean; she threw her clothes all over the room. I tried to obey the curfew rules; she sneaked out to her friend's room after lights out.

I spent many hours in class and worked long hours around the school, so we didn't see much of each other. She took several aspirins before going to bed every night. I'm sure I was the cause of it.

≈

Some things thrilled me, like the hot running water in the bathroom and the flush toilet with real toilet paper. No more newsprint pages. Each person had fresh water for her bath, too; no more dark water from bathing after another sibling.

And food—glorious food—on the table three times a day, with dessert on top of that. Mrs. Baker was a great cook and made meals she knew we students would like. The parents of some of our students lived on farms and supplied the school with beef and vegetables. Mrs. Baker made tasty roast beef and mashed potatoes. She also baked a delicious fruit cocktail cake or peanut butter cookies for dessert. I could eat as much as I liked and not go away from the table hungry.

The way I scarfed food bothered at least one other student. Our parents had never taught us any table manners, so Victoria sat beside me and tried to inject a little culture in me.

"Don't put the whole cracker in your mouth at once," she said. "Bite off a bit at a time—like this." She nibbled off a teeny corner of it.

"If my mouth is big enough to put a whole cracker in at once, what's wrong with doing it?" I asked. "You think I ain't had no fetchin' up?"[4]

She rolled her eyes and took another small bite of her cracker.

"If I ate that slow at home, my brothers would have gobbled everything before I had two bites," I said. "Pass them cookies."

"Please," she reminded me.

"Please."

"And wipe the crumbs off your mouth."

I swept them away with my sleeve.

"Good heavens! Use your napkin."

≈

I started working the first week of school. I set tables before breakfast and dinner. After each meal, I washed dishes with three other students. A senior named Joe clowned around and made all of us laugh. We had such a hoot together that we hardly considered it work. Sometimes our foolishness became so loud that Mr. Everheart had to come down from his office on the first floor and give us a warning.

"Okay, that's enough horsing around," he'd say. "You're disturbing the classes upstairs. Hold it to a low roar."

After school, while the other students relaxed and did homework in the dorm rooms, I worked in the kitchen with Mrs. Baker.

"Put these groceries away. Then you can peel this bag of potatoes."

"Heavens to Murgatroyd! How many pounds is that?"

"Twenty-five. The sooner you start, the sooner you'll be done."

I had peeled a lot of potatoes at home, as we ate them nearly every day, but never twenty-five pounds at once. Soon I became the "potato peeling queen" of Mrs. Baker's kitchen. She didn't know that I would rather do *anything* at school than be in my home. If she complimented me on my work, I tried to do it even better the next time. I soon became her most skilled helper.

When the groceries came in, I put the large cans of food away for her. I decided to be extra helpful and organize them—apples, beans, carrots.

"That's not how I told you to arrange them."

"But they're in alphabetical order."

"Take them all back off the shelf and put them the way I want them." I soon learned to do things her way.

Every so often she caught a mouse in one of the traps in the storage room. She asked me carry it outside and empty the trap. That freaked me out. I gave her a repulsed look in protest. "That's good missionary training," she said.

Okay, okay. I have to do this. Out you go, little mousey. You should have stayed out of Mrs. Baker's apple bin.

I crinkled my nose, emptied the trap and took it back in for Mrs. Baker to reset.

She preached a lot of mini-sermons to me as I worked—do all your homework, don't fool around in class, forget the boys until you're older. Goodness only knows how badly I needed some guidance. She seemed to sense my need for some tender, loving care, and often gave me a hug when I arrived to help her.

After washing the dishes from the evening meal, I swept the dining hall and made sure everything sparkled before leaving for the day. I'd be back at 6:30 the next morning to set the tables. Then I gathered up my books and went to the study hall in the library to do two hours of homework.

Mr. Morgan, the director of my work schedule, soon recognized how quickly and thoroughly I did my work and raised my wages from fifty cents an hour to fifty-five cents. It would make working off my mountain of debt a tiny bit easier. The minimum wage was a dollar an hour in 1959, but they could pay less to us students.

≈

In January of 1960, after I had been in school for a few months, I received word that my mother had gone to the hospital in Central City and given birth to my new baby sister. One of my teachers, Mrs. Stenson, offered to drive me there.

The whole idea of having another sibling didn't exactly thrill me. We had enough kids already, and my parents could barely afford to feed and clothe them. Mom would turn forty-four in a couple of weeks. Clyde would be twenty a few days after that. The thought that my parents still had sex embarrassed me to no end. Good grief! It made me ill.

When Mrs. Stenson found the room where my mother stayed, I hesitated in the doorway, my arms folded over my chest.

She touched my shoulder. "Go on in and give your mother a hug."

I dragged my feet over to the bed and gave her a quick hug.

"What did you name her?" I asked.

"Sherry, like you suggested."

I eventually came to like my baby sister, but I never really knew her like Molly, because I spent so little time at home.

≈

In my second year at Nebraska Christian, I needed a new pair of glasses. My mother came up to the school with my two little sisters and took me to the optometrist. My parents had bought my first cheap, generic-looking pair when I started the eighth grade. This time I went for something fancier, but they cost thirty-five dollars. I paid for them myself this time—except for the five dollars Mom gave me—the only money I received from her in those three years.

I asked the optometrist about payment terms. "I have two young children," he said, "and my wife and I have a hard time finding a babysitter. How would you like to take care of them on Friday nights until your glasses are paid for?"

"I'd be happy to do that," I said. "I have two younger sisters. We have lots of fun together."

"Great! Now my wife and I can go out for dinner and a movie."

It took weeks and weeks of babysitting to pay off my debt, but I had a spiffy new pair of glasses. And I felt like they were free, because I only gave him five dollars for them.

≈

During my second year at Nebraska Christian, my brother Jimmy, who had graduated from Clarks Public High School that spring, found a job in Columbus working at a garage. He fixed cars forty hours a week for a dollar an hour. After his first week on the job, he wrote to me about it.

My friend Robin stood near me in the school office when I checked my mail slot.

"Hey, I got a letter from Jimmy!" I said.

"Well, bless his heart! I wish my brothers would write to me."

I carefully unsealed the envelope. My fingers shook with excitement. As I opened it, something fell out on the floor.

I read the letter to Robin. "Dear Lizzy, Hi! How is school going? I like my new job working at this here garage in Columbus. They pay me a whole dollar an hour. Can you believe that? I made forty bucks this week. I thought you could use some help with your tuition expenses, so I'm sending you a check. Love, Jimmy."

Robin, in the meantime, picked up what had fallen on the floor and handed it to me. When I opened it, I saw a check for a whopping forty dollars.

I gasped. "He sent his whole first week's wages to me!" I burst into tears.

"What a nice brother," Robin said.

"He's my best friend in the whole world."

"I can see that."

"He's talking of joining the Navy when he turns eighteen in November. I'll sure miss him if he goes away. I wonder who will drive me back and forth to school, if he does leave."

Robin slid her arm around my shoulder. "Cross that bridge when you get to it."

I signed the back of Jimmy's check and gave it to the school secretary to apply to my account.

≈

As time went on, I started to feel better about myself. I learned to eat neatly and curled my own hair when I didn't wear it in a ponytail. I washed my clothes in a fancy automatic washer and hung them on the line to dry. My second-year roommate treated me well. I turned in my assignments on time, after working hard to perfect them. I stayed out of trouble. Actually, I didn't have time to misbehave. I had to work all the time. I loved my teachers and classmates.

Thank you, God. You have been so good to me. I want to make my life count for you. I'll do whatever you want me to do.

XXI

Learning to
Trust Mr. Everheart

BY THE TIME I REACHED MY TEENS, I HAD BUILT A THICK WALL AROUND myself so no one could come close enough to hurt me again. Unfortunately, by doing that, I kept out the good, as well as the bad. That started to change when I attended Nebraska Christian High School. It didn't take long for the superintendent, Mr. Everheart, to notice that something was drastically wrong with me.

As head of our small school, he assigned a teacher to meet one-on-one with each student once a month. Most of us roomed in the dorms away from home and sometimes needed advice from a caring adult. The person who became responsible for me turned out to be Mr. Everheart.

The first time he called me into his office, I was terrified. I hesitated in the doorway with my hands behind my back.

"Come on in and sit down," he said.

I slipped into the chair across from his desk, near the door. My eyes darted around the room. I noticed a photo of his wife and five children on the credenza behind his desk. I wondered what it would be like to belong to a happy family like theirs.

"How are your classes going?"

"Not too bad, except Home Economics. I got a B minus in that one."

"Why is that?"

"Well, I ain't never learned to cook." I looked down and shifted in my chair.

"It looks like you need some help with your English, too," he said. "In proper English, we don't say, 'ain't.'"

"What am I *supposed* to say?"

"Say, 'I haven't learned to cook.'"

I crinkled my nose. "That sounds funny. It's gonna be hard to change, but I'll try."

After a bit more chatting, I left his office and went to class.

≈

In the next session, after a few minutes of inquiring about my studies, Mr. Everheart asked about my family. I had hoped I would never have to mention them.

"Are your parents happy you're in this school?"

"I think my mom is, but my dad ain't talked to me since I left in September."

"Why is that?"

"My mom had another baby in January. He wanted me to stay home and help her. I clean the house for her when I go home on the weekend though."

He shifted in his chair and leaned forward.

"How many children are in your family?"

"My oldest brother Clyde is twenty. My next brother Jimmy is seventeen. My sister Molly is nine. Sherry is only a few months old."

"Were you excited about having a new sibling?"

"Not really," I said. "Our house ain't big enough for all them kids. Besides, they ain't got enough money to take care of us."

He stroked his chin and furrowed his brow.

"How do you feel about your family?"

I thought for a long, long time about that one.

Which part am I least ashamed of that I could tell him about? Our messy house? Our chaotic family? The beatings? The sexual abuse? How can I begin to tell him how I feel about any of it?

Would he understand that, by the time I was eight, I had noticed that only babies deserved hugs and cuddles? It hurt me to think that, somewhere along the way, I had become unlovable.

I watched my mom cradle my little sister Molly and wished I were the one in her arms. I had a deep, empty cavern in my heart. If someone would hold me, I would soak up as much love as I could. I would keep it in my heart and treasure it forever. When I noticed other mothers in church holding their babies, stroking their heads and rubbing their backs, I felt empty inside. Why didn't anyone do that to me? What must it feel like?

Had Mom left me crying in my crib when I needed to be fed, changed, or given attention? Did Mom allow Clyde to hurt me when I was little? She certainly didn't intervene when he was older. She said I cried a lot in my early years. I hate to even consider what may have caused that.

Is that why I received so many beatings—because I was unlovable? No one seemed to care about my feelings. Clyde always called me a crybaby. Mom pushed me away when I tried to hug her. Dad beat me without a smidgen of remorse—that I could see.

Why am I so disgusting to everyone, I wondered. Why am I so ashamed of who I am? Why am I such a bad girl? Can I ever learn to be better? What will it take?

I often worried that we wouldn't have enough to eat. It embarrassed me that the other kids poked fun at us because we couldn't afford better clothes. I lived in constant fear that the thudding footsteps on the stairs—or worse, the stealthy ones when Dad wanted to add to the punishment by sneaking up and bursting into my bedroom without warning—would mean another beating. I became hyper-vigilant—always on the lookout for what disaster would strike next. My personal boundaries could be crossed at any time without my permission. I not only felt terror-stricken, but also empty, disconnected and alone.

Mr. Everheart sat patiently while I mulled all this over in my mind.

"I don't really know how I feel about my family," I said slowly. Then a recent incident flashed through my mind.

Being away at school during the week didn't exempt me from obeying my dad when I returned home on weekends. Ever since I left in the fall, he looked for reasons to take out his anger on me. The slightest infraction ticked him off.

A few weeks after school started, my grandparents came for a visit from Minnesota. We all sat around the table eating supper. I had received some school news in the mail that day and, anxious to finish reading it, took it with me to the table.

Dad said, "Put that away."

I kept reading.

He yelled, "Is that what they're teaching you at that school, to disrespect your parents? I told you to put that away."

Then he proceeded to give me one of the worst spankings I'd had in a long time. He didn't take time to find the strap and starting hitting me with his hand. One, two, three, . . .

I yelled, "Stop, Daddy! Stop!"

Four, five, six, . . .

I tried to squirm out of his hold on me.

Seven, eight, nine, . . .

As I made one last effort to get away, he accidentally banged me in the eye with his elbow. I had a black eye for weeks.

Grandpa stood up. "You're too hard on that girl, Clarence."

"No, I ain't. She needs to learn a few lessons yet. She's as stubborn as a mule."

I felt so humiliated to receive a beating in front of my dear grandparents. *Now they won't love me anymore either. I wish I never had to go back home. Maybe I'll find a way to stay at my school.*

When I finally looked up, Mr. Everheart was watching me. "Is there something you want to tell me, Lizzy?"

"No, I only thought about something that happened last fall."

"Would you like talk about it?"

"Not this time." I stood up and started for the door.

"We'll talk more about it later then. Try a little harder in Home Ec. class, okay?" I paused with my hand on the doorknob. "Sure, but I ain't never gonna cook like Mrs. Stenson."

"There's that word again. Better work on that, too," he said.

"Oh, good gravy," I mumbled. I left his office and headed for the girls' bathroom. After bringing up that memory, I felt like barfing.

How can I ever tell Mr. Everheart what has been going on in my house? He seems to really care about me. Maybe I'll screw up the courage to tell him next time. Yes, I'll do that.

XXII

Letting the Story Out

A FEW WEEKS LATER, I CHECKED IN AT THE ADMINISTRATION OFFICE AND asked Miss Wilson if Mr. Everheart was expecting me. She knocked on his door, checked briefly with him and said, "Yes, go on in."

"Hi, Lizzy! Come on in," Mr. Everheart said.

I sat down in his comfortable green and white striped velvet chair.

"How are things going?"

"Oh, purdy good," I said. I glanced out the window at the snow clinging to one side of a tree.

"I looked at your records. You're doing extremely well in your studies."

I straightened up in my chair. "Thank you. I study hard after I finish working."

It felt good to have him acknowledge my success.

"So you're still happy you decided to come here?"

"Yes, I feel safe here."

"Safe? Don't you feel safe in your home?"

Uh, oh. Here goes! I'll tell him a little bit.

"Not really. My dad whips me every so often."

"You mean with his hand?"

"Sometimes. If I'm really bad, he uses a piece of old farm machinery belt. It's about a foot and a half long, two inches wide and a quarter of an inch thick. It's burnt orange, and I hate that color."

Mr. Everheart leaned forward. "He beats you with that?"

"Yeah, lots of times. I can feel the welts through my clothes when he's done with me. It takes about six weeks for the bruises to go away. He says as long as I have my feet under his table, I have to obey him."

"But why would he beat you so severely?"

"He says the Bible tells him to do so. He often quotes that verse, 'Spare the rod and spoil the child.' Otherwise, he says, I'll grow up spoiled."

"I don't think that's what that verse meant for him to do. I'm sorry, Lizzy. There's no excuse for abusing a child like that."

Why would the Bible encourage him to abuse me? I don't understand. I squirmed in my chair.

"That's abuse?" I said out loud.

"Yes, I have five children, and I don't beat them to make them obey me."

"That sounds impossible to me."

How could anyone raise children without beating them? How does he make his children obey him?

I stared out the window and tried to wrap my head around such a thought.

"Lizzy, is there any other reason you feel unsafe in your home?"

I clenched my hands in my lap and swallowed hard. "Yeah, but I can't talk about it."

"You can tell me anything you like. You're safe with me. I will keep it confidential."

He smiled at me across the desk. I could see in his eyes that he meant it.

"I know I'm safe with you, but he said he would kill me, if I ever told anyone."

"Who did?"

"My brother Clyde. He could do it, too. He stomps his feet, shakes his fists, and screams. And he throws stuff. Once he hit me in the head with a baseball and knocked me out. He bent a cake pan in half over my brother Jimmy's head. He killed my favorite kitten."

Mr. Everheart raised his eyebrows.

"What do your parents do about that?"

"Dad yells at him. Mom does nothing. I think they're afraid of him, too."

"That could be." He paused. "Lizzy, are there worse things you need to tell me about?"

I swallowed hard. I took a deep breath, hoping it wouldn't be one of my last. I stared at the floor. As terrified as I was, I was even more tired of keeping secrets. Maybe it would help to tell someone. Slowly, I lifted my head. "In one of his rages, Clyde lifted the end of my bed up and crashed it down so hard several times that it broke the metal crossbars."

"He did? Why did he do that?"

"Because I kicked him and told him to stop botherin' me. He became furious. First, he threw a Webster's dictionary at me. It missed me and hit my little sister Molly in the head. Then he came back a second time and broke my bed."

Mr. Everheart grimaced. He gripped the arms of his swivel chair. "Go ahead. What happened then?"

"My parents came running upstairs when they heard the noise. Clyde lied and made up an excuse that he couldn't get to sleep because I had my light on. I didn't want to git a beating for tellin' the truth, so I lied, too. Dad said he would beat me if he heard any more noise."

I glanced up at Mr. Everheart, took another deep breath and continued. "I tried to go to sleep, but he had broken one end of my bed. I kept sliding down to the low end of it. I finally went downstairs, woke up my dad and asked him to undo the other end and put my mattress on the floor. He came back upstairs, cursing under his breath about missing his sleep, and loosened the bars from the headboard. I still couldn't git to sleep though, not with that monster across the hall from my sister and me."

Mr. Everheart sat there looking a little stunned. "I'm beginning to see why you don't feel safe in your home. Maybe we can arrange to have you stay here at school on the weekends."

"I'll do anything—anything. I'll work all weekend, so I don't have to go home."

I hope he finds a way to let me stay here. Please, God! Please!

"Lizzy, this might be difficult for you to talk about, but it would be good to tell someone about what actually happened the night Clyde broke your bed," he said. "I really care about you and want to help you."

I've never had anyone care about me before. It seems so strange. Should I trust him? Will he tell someone else? Will he call my parents? Will he notify the police? If my dad goes to jail, who will take care of my family? What will he think when I tell him what Clyde has been doing to me? I'm so bad! So bad!

"Lizzy, you mentioned that your brother 'bothered' you. Do you mean that he touched your private parts?"

No! No! I can't tell him! It's so dirty! So disgusting! He said he would kill me if I told anyone. Mr. Everheart knows. Now I'm gonna die!

I gripped the arms of my chair until my knuckles turned white. I felt like I was about to go down a steep roller coaster. Only halfway up the other side, the ride would suddenly end—and I would be propelled off into outer darkness. *I'm gonna die! I'm gonna die!*

"It's hard to talk about, isn't it, Lizzy?"

I nodded my head. Then I pulled my knees up under my chin and clasped them tightly with my arms. I rocked back and forth. Then I started to sob uncontrollably. *I'm dead! I'm dead!*

"I'm so sorry, Lizzy," he said. "I wish I could take your bad feelings away."

When I regained my composure, I looked up and saw he had covered his face with his hands and also wept. He shared some tissues with me.

Finally, he said, "Lizzy, that's why Jesus came—to heal people like you. Could I pray with you and ask him to start doing that for you?"

I couldn't speak so I just nodded my head.

When he finished praying for me, he handed me some more tissues. "I'm here for you, Lizzy. If you need to talk, make an appointment with Miss Wilson. Anytime. If you need to go back to the dorm for a while until you feel better, I'll write a pass for you to be excused from your next class."

"Thank you. I'd better do that."

I told someone, and I'm still alive!

≈

As I walked back towards the dorm, I tried to keep the tears from coming, but they flowed down my reddened cheeks. I hoped no one would stop me and ask questions, but my dorm mother saw me coming and stepped out of her apartment to greet me.

"Hey, Lizzy, aren't you supposed to be in class?" Mrs. Spencer asked.

"Yes, but Mr. Everheart gave me a pass to go to my room for a bit."

"You've been crying, sweetheart. What's the matter? Come in and tell me what's making you so sad."

I followed her into her living room and sat beside her on the sofa. "Aren't you feeling well?"

"No, my stomach hurts. I feel like I'm gonna barf."

She brought a wastebasket and set it close by.

"Are you having trouble in school, sweetheart?"

"No, I love it here."

Mrs. Spencer went to the kitchen and fetched a plate of chocolate chip cookies. After a few bites, I started to feel better.

She patted my knee. "If you don't feel like talking about it now, that's okay, but I'm here whenever you want."

"Thanks, Mrs. Spencer."

As I rose to leave, she put her arms around me and gave me one of the first caring hugs I had ever had in my life. I had only known mostly "bad touch" until Nebraska Christian High School.

My own mother shoved me away when I tried to put my arm around her neck as she sat at the table. "Git off of me," she said. When I asked her to give me a kiss and hug at bedtime, like my friends received, she said, "You're too big for that."

Mrs. Spencer's hug was incredible. I let her hold me for a long time while I wept. It became one of the first few drops of rain on the desert of my heart.

As I left, she said, "You can come back for another hug whenever you like. Maybe you can tell me what makes you so sad."

I headed for my room to process what had happened to me that day. The truth that I didn't deserve all the abuse that happened to me slowly worked its way into my consciousness. I had loosened one tyrannical rope from around my heart. If I lived through that, maybe I could one day be free.

I also experienced what it felt like to be loved. It had taken me fifteen years to find out. My heart felt so warm, I must have glowed in the dark for a few days.

The wall around me started to crumble—and I didn't even want to build it back up.

XXIII

Music Cheered Me

SOMEONE GAVE OUR FAMILY AN OLD CLUNKER OF A PIANO. I TRIED AND tried on my own to play a hymn on it, but it sounded horrible. (And not only because it hadn't been tuned for a long time.) One day I asked my mother, "Can I find someone to teach me to play this piano?"

"How much do lessons cost?" she asked.

"A dollar for a half-hour lesson."

"A whole dollar? Do you think money grows on trees? Your daddy only makes a hundred and fifty dollars a month. Four dollars buys a lot of groceries."

"Okay, I'll see if I can git some lessons at school."

I started taking free snare drum lessons from the music teacher at the little school in Clarks in the eighth grade. I couldn't take the drum home from school, so I practiced on a little square rubber pad. I could pound out a lot of frustration on that thing. I learned to play flamadiddles, paradiddles and several marching cadences.

I joined the marching band and played at halftime at football games. It took a lot of practice to keep us all going in the right direction while playing our music. I especially loved the Sousa marches. They stirred my soul.

I thought I looked spiffy in my royal blue band uniform. I somehow felt like a different person all dressed up like that. In the fall of each year, we marched in the parade in Grand Island. By the end of the route, I had blisters on my feet and could barely walk. We didn't win any awards, but we sure had fun.

When I changed schools from Clarks Public to Nebraska Christian in the tenth grade, I continued to play the snare and bass drum for a year. One day I asked Mr. Spencer, the music teacher at Nebraska Christian, if I could play a different instrument.

"There's an old French horn in the music room that no one uses. Do you want to try that?"

"Sure," I said. I had played the e-flat alto horn for a short time in my previous school, so I quickly adapted my skills to this instrument, although I had to play the keys with my left hand instead of my right. I liked the melancholy sound of the French horn and soon I was playing it in the school band.

Music reverberated through my mind and heart all day. It chased away my sadness and filled my heart with joy.

In my last year of high school, I saw one of the boys playing a trombone. One day I asked him if I could borrow it and he showed me how to push the slide back and forth. "Be careful not to let go of the slide. If it gets bent, it won't work anymore."

"I'll be careful."

I took it to Mr. Spencer. "Can you teach me how to play this?"

"Another instrument?"

I don't remember how much the lessons cost, but I came up with enough money from shining my dorm mate's shoes for ten cents a pair to pay for six of them.

When students started practicing for the spring music festival, I asked Mr. Spencer if my friend Susan and I could play a trombone duet for it.

"You've only had six lessons," he said.

"I know, but I want to at least try."

He rubbed his nose. "Okay, I'll give you a fairly easy song to learn. The adjudicator might mark you down for that, though."

"That's okay. The easier, the better."

"The deal is you have to practice it fifty times. If you do that, I'll let you go."

"Lizzy" and "Susan" practicing for the music festival with "Mr. Spencer"

Susan and I practiced *On Wings of Song*, composed by Felix Mendelssohn, day after day. Mr. Spencer listened to us one afternoon, after we had practiced it at least fifty times. "Okay, you can go to the festival, but don't get your hopes up too high. Have fun. That's all."

Suddenly, we started to panic. We would have to stand in front of the judges and play our song from memory—with Mr. Spencer watching, too.

One of the other students with a good sense of humor overheard us talking about how worried we were. "You know how I overcome my fright?"

"How?"

"I imagine the judges wearing long red underwear."

"Really?" I asked. "I'm gonna try that."

When it was our turn to play at the festival, Susan and I smiled at each other. We knew what the other was imagining, and relaxed enough at the thought to play the song better than we ever did in practice.

When we finished, the judge announced his ruling. "That wasn't a complicated piece, but the way you sustained those high notes impressed me, Lizzy. I'm giving you a superior rating."

Superior? The highest rating possible? Unbelievable! Our jaws dropped. Mr. Spencer grinned when he saw the shocked look on our faces. We went home from the festival elated.

I raced into the kitchen after school, waving my certificate.

"How did your duet go?" Mrs. Baker asked.

"He gave us a superior! We didn't expect that."

"What a nice surprise." She gave me a big hug.

≈

I also sang alto in the school choir, which often went around to churches in the area and put on programs to raise money for the school.

During the program, Mr. Spencer gave some of us choir members a chance to give a testimony of how God had blessed us. Though self-conscious and apprehensive, I recounted how much I appreciated God making it possible for me to go to Nebraska Christian.

We didn't have a bus, so the teachers had to transport us. On the way home from one of the tours, I rode in a car with Mr. Everheart and the male quartet.

Those guys not only sang well, but also had a great sense of humor. Along the way, they spontaneously started to sing, *Ezekiel's Dry Bones.* "The toe bone's connected to the foot bone." Then one of them would make hilarious sound effects to match each connection. They continued on up the skeleton, "Foot bone connected to the heel bone, DING! heel bone connected to the ankle bone, PLINK! ankle bone connected to the shin bone, BEEP! shin bone connected to the knee bone, PIP! knee bone connected to the back bone, BONK! back bone connected to the shoulder bone, THUNK! shoulder bone connected to the neck bone, BLIP! neck bone connected to the head bone, WHUMP! Now hear the word of the Lord." They had Mr. Everheart and me in stitches. Then they sang it all backwards from the head to the toe with more sound effects. It made the ride back to school go quickly.

≈

Since our school's music program excelled, we almost always received superior ratings for each entry in the festivals. One judge said we sang like we meant it. We had a strong faith in God and loved to sing about it. Besides, Mr. Spencer did an incredible job as our music teacher. He taught us to choose wisely what we could sing with conviction from our hearts, and then to perform to the best of our ability.

One time while he directed our choir, one of the students noticed the button on his suit jacket hung by a thread and threatened to fly off at any moment. As the students whispered the news from one to another, we could barely sing anymore. Finally, he stopped directing and said, "Okay, what's so funny?"

No one wanted to say.

"We're not going on until you tell me."

"The button on your coat sleeve is loose," Jenny said. "We're waiting for it to go flying."

He ripped it off and put it in his pocket. Mrs. Spencer would have to sew it back on. We continued singing, now in a much lighter mood. The music continued to echo through my soul the rest of the day.

XXIV

The Last Straw

In the summer between my junior and senior years, I turned seventeen and started to look forward to going back to finish high school. I loved my teachers and had made many good friends there, especially Robin. She came from the northern part of the state and had grown up in circumstances similar to mine. She was easy-going and accepted me without a hint of judgment. We laughed and cried and prayed together.

Soon I would graduate and be able to leave home for good. I couldn't wait. I tried to work as many hours away from home as possible in the summer so I wouldn't have to encounter my brother Clyde. I wished he would leave home. Even though he didn't touch me after I turned fourteen, the leers he gave me made me feel disgusting and uncomfortable. Jimmy had enlisted in the U.S. Navy in November of my junior year. Why couldn't Clyde go?

I not only worked at the motel, but also volunteered for any task at Nebraska Christian that I could do for a few extra dollars. The school was located thirteen miles from my home, so I had two ways to get there, either hitchhike or ride my bicycle.

Since I worked at the gas station for Mr. Jansen, he would wait until a kindhearted couple came along to fill up their tank, and then ask them if they would mind dropping me off in the next town. They would take me to within two miles of my school. I walked the rest of the way.

Thoughts of Charles Starkweather were always at the top of my mind. He had gone on a two-month murder spree in Nebraska and Wyoming, between December of 1957 and January of 1958, and killed eleven people. The state executed him in the electric chair seventeen months later. Though he was now dead, I took extra care when I travelled alone. I didn't want to end up a murder victim.

If I went by bicycle, I rode a quarter of a mile to U.S. Highway 30, then eleven miles on the highway to Central City, plus another two miles through the town and out to the school. I tried to watch for the huge trucks coming and ride off to the side while they passed. Sometimes they nearly blew me into the ditch.

What a crazy idea to ride my bike to the school. These trucks could wipe me off the map in one swift blow. But what choice do I have? I need to earn money to go back to school.

It's hot in Nebraska in mid-summer—90° to 100°F (32° to 38° Celsius)—in the shade. I took a little jar of water along and stopped to take a sip every mile or so.

If a truck don't smack into me, then I'll die of thirst. How will I ever be able to work after I arrive? I'm plum wore out, and I still have three miles to go.

When I arrived at school, Miss Kruger met me at the front door.

"You made it, but your face is all red," she said. "It's too hot to be riding that far."

"I know, but I couldn't find a ride with anyone, and I ran out of water along the way."

She let me rest for a few minutes, and I drank some water from the drinking fountain before I started working.

Thank you, Lord, for getting me here safely. Now I need strength to work.

The administration building had belonged to Nebraska Central College, operated by the Society of Friends, or Quakers, from 1899 to 1953. It stood idle until a group of concerned parents purchased it and opened our high school there in 1959.

Miss Kruger, the librarian, asked me to catalogue all the old periodicals up in the attic.

"The historical society wants to know which ones we have and how many of each copy," she said. "They're in the attic, up in the bell tower."

We went upstairs to the second floor of the building and then climbed a narrow, creaky stairway up to the bell tower. When I saw

The steep ladder to the attic

the steep ladder I had to climb to get to the attic opening in the ceiling, I nearly fainted.

Oh, no! I can't do this. I can't do this. It's at least 12 feet up the ladder to the attic. Below the ladder, I could fall another 15 feet to the floor. I can't have survived the trek to school, only to plunge to my death from a rickety old ladder. Oh, oh, oh!

Miss Kruger saw me hesitate. "What's the matter?"

"I don't know if I can do this. I'm afraid of heights," I said. "My brother Clyde made me climb up a steep ladder in our silo once. It scared me so bad, I vowed never to climb up high again."

I noticed the worried look on her face. It must have been a reflection of my own.

"I'll hold the bottom of the ladder so it doesn't slip," she said.

"Ain't there no other way to do this?"

"I'm afraid not. Go on up. I'll watch you."

That's easy for her to say. I'm the one on this precarious ladder.

I ascended one cautious step after another.

148

Don't look down. Lord, help me not to fall.

I eventually made it to the top, pulled myself up into the attic and sat near the edge of the opening. I reached over in the semi-darkness, picked up a pile, blew off the dust and counted the periodicals. Down below, Miss Kruger recorded the information in her notebook.

"Seven copies of the *Friends' Journal*," I hollered.

"Okay, what's next?"

"Thirteen copies of the *Quaker Monthly*."

After a couple of hours, I finished all the piles within reach.

"Now I have to git back down."

"I'll hold the ladder again. Come on down."

"Is there a prize if I make it down in one piece?"

She chuckled. "Yes, I'll share my lunch with you."

I turned around backwards and knelt near the opening. I felt for the first rung on the ladder with my right foot. After making a few attempts and finding only thin air, I finally touched the step. Then I slowly descended one apprehensive step at a time. When I reached the landing, I sat on the top step of the stairway for a minute to dry my sweaty palms and regain my composure.

"Are you okay?" Miss Kruger asked.

"I will be, when I stop shaking."

It took several days to complete the cataloguing. Despite my fear, I came to help whenever I could.

≈

The next time I went to help Miss Kruger, I had a problem. I decided to go by bicycle again, rather than try to hitch a ride. I packed a sandwich and a jar of water for the trip. When I had everything gathered together to leave, I grabbed the bag and went out to put it in the wire basket on the front of my bicycle. But I found the whole thing turned upside down—with the rear tire removed. Clyde, grinning, stood near it.

"Why in the heck did you take my bike apart?" I screamed. "I have to go to work."

"It had a flat tire," he said.

"Well, hurry up and fix it."

Furious, I stomped my foot and kicked dirt at him.

"I can't. This tube is busted, and I ain't got no new one."

"How am I s'posed to git to work?"

"That's your problem."

"Darn you! When are you ever going to stop tormentin' me? Why don't you git out of our house and stay out?"

I had to call the school and tell them I couldn't come or they might have thought I had met with some misfortune along the way—a high possibility.

Miss Wilson, the school secretary, answered the phone. "Nebraska Christian High School. How may I help you?"

"It's me—Lizzy Bauman. I was s'posed to help Miss Kruger today. Could you tell her I couldn't find a ride, please?"

"Okay, Lizzy. She came into the office a few minutes ago wondering why you hadn't shown up. I'll tell her."

"Thanks, Miss Wilson. I'll come again when my bicycle gits fixed."

When our family met for dinner at noon, Clyde sat on one end of the bench and I sat on the other. My parents and youngest sister Sherry sat across the table from us. Molly sat at the end of the table near me. Jimmy was away in the Navy.

I still seethed from the morning's catastrophe.

I glanced at Clyde. He was eating his potatoes after putting way too much ketchup on them.

Mom fed Sherry. Dad looked weary after a hard morning of work.

"Miss Kruger expected me to work at the school today," I said.

"So, why didn't you go?" Dad asked.

"Clyde took my bike apart and won't put it back together."

"I'll fix it next week when I git a new tube," Clyde said.

I banged my fist on the table. "But I need it *now*, not a week from now."

The argument went back and forth until I'd finally had enough. Frustrated and furious, I raised my hand and smacked my fist into

Clyde's face. I was surprised when my hand connected and his nose started to bleed.

Dad saw the blood and charged off to the porch. I couldn't find the strength to run away.

My mother stood up and slumped silently behind her chair. My sisters sat wide-eyed, hands over their ears and fear etched on their faces.

Dad returned with the machinery belt. He bent me over and started hitting me on my behind with it.

Whack! Whack! Whack!

I screamed and tried to get away. "Stop, Daddy, stop!" He continued to hit me on my bum and legs. I tried to cover myself with my hands, but the lashes hurt there even more.

After he hit me about ten times, he paused. "That'll teach you a lesson, Girl."

I spun around and planted my open hands firmly on his chest and shoved him backwards. "You ain't teachin' me *nuthin*!" Then I tried to run.

That did it. He grabbed my arm, bent me over and hit me at least fifteen more times on my rear before he ran out of steam.

I walked over to my mom, tears streaming down my face.

"You deserved that." She turned away. "That's no way to talk to your dad."

I turned around and dragged myself up to my bedroom. I tried to sit on the edge of the bed, but that hurt too much. I could feel the welts welling up through my clothes.

I slowly peeled off my dress and underskirt. Oh, it hurt. It felt like my skin was on fire.

I turned around and looked in the mirror on my dresser. I was covered with wide red stripes from my waist to my knees. I was surprised they weren't bleeding. Dad had never hit me that hard, or that many times, before.

I lay down and cried for a long time.

I am so bad—so, so bad.

Then something welled up in me that I had never felt before. I stopped crying, gritted my teeth and vowed a lot of hateful things that day.

I'm not bad. He is. I'm gittin' out of this place. I will never come home again. I hate my dad for beating me all the time. I hate my mom for having no sympathy for me. I hate Clyde for torturing me all the time. I'm done with this. Lord, have mercy on me.

My heart filled with many more dark spots that day. I started to build a new thick wall around myself. No one would ever hurt me again.

≈

A few days later, I caught a ride up to the school with a tourist from the filling station.

Miss Wilson and Mr. Everheart greeted me when I walked in with my head down.

"Miss Kruger was worried about you when you didn't show up the other day," Mr. Everheart said. "What happened?"

"My brother Clyde and I got into a fight," I said. "I got mad and hit him in the face. My dad beat me for it."

"He beat you again?" Mr. Everheart asked.

This time I knew it was safe to share. "Yeah, do you want to see what he did to me?" I lifted up my skirt a few inches and showed them the mass of bruises that colored my thighs.

Miss Wilson gasped and turned away. Mr. Everheart covered his face with his hands. "I'm so sorry, Lizzy." Then he put his arm around me and I cried on his shoulder.

"I wish there was something we could do to get you out of that home," Mr. Everheart said.

≈

A few weeks later, at the beginning of my final year, Mr. Everheart called me into his office.

"Lizzy, I know how dangerous it is for you to go home on weekends. How would you like to stay here at school? We need someone to clean the administration building on Saturdays. You could earn some extra money to pay off your account. What do you think?"

I smiled and clasped my hands together in front of my chest. "Oh, could I? I'll clean for as long as you want, if only I don't have to go home."

"Mr. Morgan is in charge of maintenance. He'll get you started on your jobs this weekend."

"Thanks a million, Mr. Everheart."

I squealed and skipped out of his office, then ran straight to the dorm to tell Robin my news. She hugged me, and we did a little jig in the middle of the hallway.

On Saturday morning, Mr. Morgan gave me a list of jobs to do—wash the classroom floors and buff them with a machine, wipe the blackboards, clean all the stairways and sanitize both the boys' and girls' bathrooms. My pay rate would remain at fifty-five cents an hour. Terrific!

I sang through my duties. My favorite song was an old hymn I had learned in church—*Count Your Blessings.*

Are you ever burdened with a load of care?
Does the cross seem heavy you are called to bear?
Count your many blessings; every doubt will fly,
And you will keep singing as the days go by.

Count your blessings, name them one by one,
Count your blessings, see what God has done!
Count your blessings, name them one by one,
And it will surprise you what the Lord has done.

I couldn't have been happier. My blessings started piling up. I worked about twenty hours a week, which enabled me to pay off eleven dollars of my five-hundred-dollar-debt. Who wouldn't be happy?

I didn't go home on weekends my entire senior year. For Thanksgiving, and all but two days of the Christmas holidays, I stayed with friends or with my pastor and his wife, who had now moved to Iowa. I felt much safer there.

≈

One day, near the end of the school year, Mr. Everheart called me in to the main office where he and the business manager, Mr. Baker, stood with serious expressions on their faces. They explained that I couldn't graduate until I had paid my bill in full.

My heart sank. My mouth fell open. I suddenly found it difficult to breathe.

"Can't graduate? What do you mean?" I asked. "Can't I pay it off in the summer?"

"No, you need to pay it before the end of the school year."

How can I have come this far and not graduate? There has to be a way.

"We thought it was only fair to warn you."

I straightened up and clasped my hands behind me. "I'll find a way."

He nodded. "Good."

I picked up my books. "You know, I have a heavenly Father who loves me and will take care of me." Without another word, I turned and left the office.

I went back to the dorm and told my close friends. They promised to pray that God would somehow provide the money to pay my debt, so I could graduate with them.

Robin grabbed my hand and dragged me down to room one, used for storing extra mattresses. We knelt and stormed heaven for an answer.

Dear God, I can't work any more hours. I wouldn't have time to study, if I did. Final exams are coming up soon. If I don't come up with some money, I can't graduate. Please help me, God. I leave it with you and trust you to provide for me.

I picked up my load of books, which seemed almost as heavy as my heart, and headed for the library to study with Robin.

XXV

Life-Changing Courses

ONE OF MY FAVORITE COURSES IN HIGH SCHOOL WAS SPANISH. I HAD long dreamed of going to South America as a missionary. Our teacher, Mr. Rodriguez, taught his native language with enthusiasm, and I took to learning Spanish like a thirsty deer to a babbling brook. Soon I could speak a few sentences. I practiced after school on Mrs. Baker, who had been a missionary in Central America.

In my final year, I also took a Bible course on the New Testament book of Romans, a letter written by the Apostle Paul. Mr. Baker, whose wife I worked for in the kitchen, and who had been a pastor and missionary, taught the class. One day he pointed out Romans 3:12, "There is no one who does good, not even one," and 3:23, "For all have sinned and fall short of the glory of God."

Well, he didn't need to persuade me that I had sinned against God. Even though I thought I had been unfairly punished by my earthly father and carried false guilt from the abuse I had suffered from Clyde, I knew in my heart that I had committed other sins. I felt strong hatred, bitterness, anger and resentment toward some of my family members. I didn't always obey my mother's orders. And I had lied numerous times to avoid punishment.

In another class, he taught Romans 6:23, "For the wages of sin is death, . . ."

So my punishment isn't merely gittin' a whippin'. In God's books, it's eternal death—separation from God forever. That's a tough one to swallow.

"However," Mr. Baker continued, "the end of that verse says, 'but the gift of God is eternal life in Christ Jesus our Lord.'"

Oh, so there's a way out? God will give me eternal life if I believe in what his son Jesus did for me on the cross?

The following class he taught us Romans 5:8, which says, "But God demonstrates his own love for us in this: While we were still *sinners*, Christ died for us."

He didn't wait for me to be good or to git my life straightened out. He died for me when I was a rotten sinner. I'm grateful for that. Thank you, Jesus, for dying for me.

In another class, Mr. Baker taught us from Romans 7:15 which described the Apostle Paul's struggle with trying to do good, but doing the opposite. "I do not understand what I do. For what I want to do, I do not do, but what I hate, I do."

My ears perked up at that.

Yes, that's my struggle every day. I try not to hate, but I hate anyway. I try to forgive, but I can't. I know I should honor my parents, but it's so difficult. I withhold love from a lot of people I'm supposed to love. Was there hope for the Apostle Paul? Is there any hope for me?

What really excited me came in Romans 8:1. "Therefore, there is now no condemnation for those who are in Christ Jesus, because through Christ Jesus the law of the Spirit who gives life set you free from the law of sin and death."

I've been set free! I don't have to be eternally separated from God for my sin.

And to top that off, verses 8:37-39 held more good news. "No, in all these things we are more than conquerors through him who loved us. For I am convinced that neither death nor life, neither angels nor demons, neither the present nor the future, nor any powers, neither height nor depth, nor anything else in all creation, will be able to separate us from the love of God that is in Christ Jesus our Lord."

God loves me, and nothing in the universe can separate me from that love. I will hang on to that.

I wanted to know more about that love. I now believed I had a Father who longed to forgive me and to bind up my wounds. He wanted to strengthen me with courage. Maybe he could take away all the dark spots in my heart. One day, maybe, I could sing the last verses of *Just As I Am*.

Just as I am, you will receive,
Will welcome, pardon, cleanse, relieve;
Because your promise I believe,
O Lamb of God, I come, I come.

Just as I am, your love unknown
Has broken every barrier down;
Now, to be yours, yes, yours alone,
O Lamb of God, I come, I come.

≈

At my next counseling session with Mr. Everheart, I told him what I had been learning in my Romans class.

"I think God really does love me."

"Of course he does. What did you think he was like?"

"I thought he was like my father. That he was waiting for me to slip up so he could punish me."

He stroked his chin and thought for a moment.

"I have an assignment for you," he said. "See if you can find out what God's character is like. I want you to especially look for examples in the Bible that show he's merciful to people, even when they do wrong."

I could hardly wait to start that new project.

Not long after that, I stopped by Mr. Everheart's office and showed him my notebook with pages and pages of what I had found.

"I started digging in the book of Genesis and read to the book of Joshua before I was thoroughly convinced that God is merciful," I said. "The story about Cain, Adam and Eve's son, who killed his younger brother Abel, really surprised me. I thought God would destroy him after what he did, but you know what? God put a hedge around him, so he would be protected. Ain't that somethin'?"

"That's absolutely right. What else did you find?"

"Well, there's those nasty brothers of Joseph who sold him into slavery in Egypt. They lied to their father and said a wild animal had killed him. Years later, Joseph became a big shot and was able to help the Egyptians get through a famine. When his brothers came to Egypt to beg for food, Joseph recognized them, but they didn't know him. When his brothers finally discovered it was Joseph, they were afraid he would pay them back for all the wrongs they had done to him. Instead, he showed them kindness." I read out of my notes, "You intended to harm me, but God intended it for good to accomplish what is now being done, the saving of many lives. So then, don't be afraid."

"Lizzy, I think you've discovered an important principle," Mr. Everheart said. "Your family has done great harm to you, but God can use your experience to help other people. Do you believe that?"

"I hope so. I wouldn't want all that pain to be wasted. Maybe I *will* help someone when I tell them my story of how God rescued me from my home."

"I'm sure you will. I can see God's hand on your life. You are one special young lady."

"Thank you." I was smiling when I left for my next class.

Mr. Everheart thinks God can use me to help others. That's cool. But will I ever be brave enough to tell other people? It took me sixteen years to tell even one person.

Dear God, it's me, Lizzy again. If you want me to help other people, I need to git rid of all these dark spots in my heart. If you can do that for me, then I'll know for sure you can do it for others. Is there a way? Just askin'.

XXVI

Getting Rid of the Dark Spots

On a heavenly cloudless day, shortly before graduation in May of 1962, Mr. Everheart called me into his office for one last counseling session. He smiled at me from behind his large oak desk. I plunked down in my favorite chair with the green and white striped velvet seat cushion.

"Your time is almost finished here at Nebraska Christian, and you'll soon be going on to Bible College. How do you feel about that?"

"These past three years have been the most amazing ones of my life," I said. I took a deep breath and blurted out my appreciation. "Thank you for accepting me when I had next to no money. Thank you for letting me work to pay off my tuition fees." I faltered, as I tried to remember the words I'd rehearsed. "And thank you for helping me to escape from my abusive home. I will forever be grateful for that."

"You're welcome." His eyes twinkled. "You have been one of our model students—in your work ethic, your academic achievements and your strong faith in God. You have been an inspiration to me, the rest of the staff and the other students."

I beamed and wiped away a tear.

"Thank you, Mr. Everheart. I'd hate to think where I'd be today without the help I've received from this school, and especially from my talks with you. I owe a great debt of gratitude to you—and to God."

"Since this is our last session, is there anything you'd still like to discuss?"

I shifted in my chair and stared out the window behind Mr. Everheart's desk. This was my last chance to ask him about something that had bothered me for many years.

Will he have an answer for me? Can I find relief from my inner torment?

"Yes, there is something, but I don't know how to explain it." I tugged on my right ear. "When I do something wrong, I confess it to God and ask him to forgive me, and I do feel forgiven. But I also feel like I have a bunch of dark spots in my heart that won't go away, no matter what I try. After going to the altar for prayer, which I've done many times, I always return with them still in my heart."

Mr. Everheart stroked his chin, thought for a minute then leaned forward. "What you said is true. I John 1:9 says, 'If we confess our sins, he is faithful and just and will forgive us our sins and purify us from all unrighteousness.'" He paused for a moment. "But Jesus also came to heal us of the sins *others* have committed against *us*."

It was like a light bulb suddenly went on in my head. "Do you think those dark spots are from what other people did to me?"

Mr. Everheart looked at me. "What do you think?"

I thought for a while. Then I nodded slowly. "That's why I can't get rid of them myself. I thought nothing could be done about them."

Mr. Everheart smiled gently. "That's why Jesus came. Psalm 147:3 says, 'He heals the brokenhearted and binds up their wounds.' You have a lot of wounds, or dark spots, as you call them, from the neglect, beatings and sexual abuse you suffered in your home. Would you like to go to him and have him heal you?"

This sounds too good to be true. I have no idea how Jesus will do that. What if it doesn't work? But what do I have to lose?

"Okay, what do I have to do?"

"I want you to close your eyes and imagine yourself as a young child. I'll guide you to the palace where Jesus lives. Then you can go into the room where he sits and talk to him. You can tell him what your family has done to you. Are you okay with that?"

"Yes, but it sounds a bit scary." I wrapped my arms around myself. "Can I take along the book I've been writin' in about what happened

160

to me? I carry it with me all the time, 'cause I'm always gittin' into trouble."

"Certainly," he said.

My hands started to sweat. I wiped them on my skirt, and then clutched my necklace for comfort.

What if I can't find him in a big place like heaven? Will He know me? Will He have time to talk to me? Can He really git rid of my dark spots?

"I'll be close by, Lizzy. If you run into any trouble, just open your eyes."

"Okay, I'm ready." I took an extra deep breath.

"Close your eyes now and try to imagine this scene. You are about to go on a short visit to the palace where Jesus lives. As you walk along, notice how you're feeling inside."

This is a bit scary, but also exciting. I wonder if Jesus will talk to a little girl like me? I wonder if He looks like the pictures I've seen of him. Will I come close enough to touch him?

Once again my hands started to sweat. I jammed my fists into my armpits and held on for dear life.

Mr. Everheart continued. "Notice where you're walking. Feel the smooth, warm surface of the golden bricks on your bare feet."

Wow! Ain't this amazing? I'm seven years old again. My feet are dirty. I'm gonna git into trouble for leavin' footprints on this dazzlin' road.

"Look up and see the colorful flowers on either side," Mr. Everheart said.

I've never seen so many flowerbeds before. Millions of pansies, tulips, roses. My favorites.

I stop and stick my nose into a fragrant flower and take a deep sniff. The scent stays with me as I continue to walk.

"Listen to the songbirds as they fill the air with their cheerful singing."

You sure know how to sing, little birdies. And your feathers are gorgeous.

"Up ahead is the King's palace. It's *so* beautiful! Quicken your pace. Run if you like. Let the thought of seeing him fill you with hope."

I wonder how close I can come to him. I wonder what he'll say when he sees me. How will I tell him about all the things that happened to me? Should I show him my book?

"When you finally arrive at the gate of the palace, your heart sinks. Two guards with long, sharp swords stand in front of the double doors. One says, 'What are you doing here, little girl? Only the children of the king can come in here.'"

Okay, these big guys ain't gonna let me in. Now what?

"You back up a step or two and try to say as bravely as you can, 'I *am* a child of the King. He said I could come and see him whenever I wanted to.'"

In my mind, I repeated what Mr. Everheart had told me to say.

"Your heart pounds like crazy while you wait for their response. They look at each other for a moment, lower their swords, and open the immense jewel-studded doors to let you pass through."

Whew! I'm in! I didn't think they would let me.

"But then you look down the long hallway and become even more scared. It seems endless. Your heart pounds twice as fast. Your hands start to sweat," Mr. Everheart says.

How do I know where to go? What if I can't find him?

"You tiptoe down the hall. Notice the coolness of the stone floor on your feet. As you round the last corner, you see a bright light filtering out into the hallway. You creep close to the entrance and take a quick peek around the corner. It's the biggest, brightest, most awesome room you've ever seen."

Wow! My eyes ain't never gazed on nothin' like that. He's in there. He's really in there!

"You pull back around the corner for a moment."

I wish my heart would stop poundin'. This is way too excitin'.

"A chorus of angels whisper-sing inside the room. Now that you've arrived this close, you might begin to doubt."

No kidding! Why did I try to come here? Why should he care about me? I must have been dreaming to think I could come this close to him. Besides, look at me. I'm a mess. My hands are filthy. My feet are muddy. My dress is ripped. I must have slobbered down the front of it during breakfast. I should have cleaned myself up before coming.

"You can continue on in your own imagination, Lizzy, if you like," Mr. Everheart said.

My curiosity causes me to peek around the corner again. I can see Jesus sitting there. He wears a shiny white linen robe with a golden sash across his chest. His head is bowed and he seems to be praying.

Suddenly, Jesus looks up and sees me. He waves me over. The angels file out of the room, and I am alone with him. My heart races again as I inch my way across the room and approach the throne where he sits. My face is down. I'm afraid to look directly at him.

Jesus says, "Hello, Elizabeth."

"You know my name?" I look up in surprise, and he's smiling at me.

"Of course I do, my child. I was praying just now that you would come and see me today. Come closer, so I can have a good look at you."

He prays for me? He wants to see me?

As I come closer, He stands up, and then kneels in front of me, so we can be face to face.

"Hello, little one. I'm so glad you came to see me."

I stare at my dirty hands and cram them behind my back.

He tucks his finger under my chin and gently lifts up my head with more care than I've ever felt. His beautiful brown eyes and warm smile melt my heart. I start to feel better.

"If you'd like, you can come and sit on my lap, so we can have a little talk."

Sit on his lap? I gulped. *My parents didn't let me sit on theirs—but it seems to be okay here.*

I hesitate for a moment and then stretch up my arms. He picks me up, sits down and sets me on his lap. Without thinking, I reach out and rub my fingers over the soft white linen sleeve on his robe, but pull back when I realize how grubby my hands are.

He puts his arms around me and holds my head tightly against His chest for a long time. I can hear his heartbeat—thump, thump, thump. He gently kisses the top of my head.

This feels so warm and peaceful. Why hasn't anyone ever done this to me before?

Jesus says, "I'm glad you came to see me. What's troubling you?"

Now is my chance to ask him about the dark spots in my heart. Should I?

I decide to chance it.

"I have all these dark spots in my heart and I can't git rid of them."

"How did you receive those spots, Lizzy?"

"I know God said I should honor my father and mother, but it's really hard to do. My father has beaten me many times with a strap, until it makes bruises on my legs. I try to be close to my mother, but she pushes me away and says I deserve the beatings. The blackest spots come from my brother Clyde. If you've been watching, you've seen what he's done to me. I feel so dirty. I've been writing all these things in this little book."

"Could I look at it?"

I hesitate, because it contains the worst, most horrible things in my life. But Jesus looks so kind. I know he will understand.

"Okay, I trust you."

As he reads page after page, I see sadness, and sometimes anger, on his face. When he finishes, he slowly closes the book and gives me another long hug. "I'm sorry."

"Will I ever git rid of the dark spots in my heart?" Tears stream down my face.

"Those aren't dark spots, as you call them. Those are deep wounds."

"Wounds?" *Yes, that's what they feel like. They hurt so much.*

"Dark spots can be washed away, but wounds need inner healing. Is that what you want today?"

"Yes, Jesus. Please heal me."

I lean close to him again for another hug.

When I straighten up, He shows me his hands. "Look, Elizabeth. Do you see these scars?"

"Yes."

"Those are the wounds I received when the Roman soldiers nailed my hands to the cross."

Hearing about that in Sunday school is one thing, but seeing them takes my breath away.

"Go ahead. You can touch them, because they don't hurt anymore."

I rub my fingers over his scarred hands. The depth of them surprises me. I squeeze his hand between both of mine. "That must have hurt horribly."

"Yes, it did. Do you know why I let them do that to me?"

"No, why?"

"I was wounded for you, Elizabeth. I did it so I could heal *your* wounded heart. Whenever I see my scars, I think of you, my precious child."

Jesus hugging Lizzy and healing her wounded heart

He did it for me? To heal my wounds? It's confusing, but I think I understand.

"Thank you, Jesus, for dying for me," I whisper.

Jesus smiles. "You're welcome. I did it willingly, because I love you."

"I love you, too." I fling my arms around his neck and receive a warm hug in return.

"I'm so glad you came to see me today. You will come again soon, won't you?"

"Yes, I will."

I slip off his lap and suddenly notice my hands look squeaky clean. The mud between my toes is gone. Not only does my dress look clean, but also brand new, without a single rip. My eyes widen. I slap my hands against my cheeks.

"I'm spotless! I'm clean! I thought if I touched your robe, I would git it dirty, but instead, your touch made me clean."

Jesus' eyes sparkle. "Yes, that's the way my healing power works. Tell all your friends about me. I know a lot of them are hurting, too."

"I will. I'm so glad I came today. You finally took care of my dark spots."

"Your heart is meant to be clean. If anything bad happens, come back and I will purify you. You're always welcome here."

"Thank you."

I start to back away.

"I have something else for you," he says.

"What's that?"

"It's a brand new book for you to keep track of all the times I bless your life."

I look at the book in my hands. A field of red and purple fuchsia flowers decorates the aqua-colored cover. Inside he has written two things:

1. *Love me with all your heart, soul, mind and strength.*
2. *Love other people deeply from your heart, and treat them as you would like to be treated.*

"Thank you, Jesus." I give him one last hug, wave good-bye and start for home. I feel so light my feet barely touch the stone floor as I race down the hall. I reach the palace doors at such speed that, as I fly through them, I knock the guards off balance. When I glance back, I see them chuckling.

I skip over the golden bricks with my new book under my arm, and I notice the sun shining on the road, making it shimmer. "Wow! It's brilliant!"

I hurry to return, but when I see the yellow roses, I stop for a moment and take another whiff. So fragrant! I wonder if I should pick one for Mr. Everheart—but I don't.

The birds twitter a sweet tune I've never heard before. I wave and smile at them.

As I skip along the road with my newly healed heart, I sing a song we learned at school.

Shackled by a heavy burden,
'Neath a load of guilt and shame.
Then the hand of Jesus touched me,
And now I am no longer the same.

He touched me; oh, he touched me,
And oh the joy that floods my soul!
Something happened and now I know,
He touched me and made me whole.

Since I met this blessed Savior,
Since he cleansed and made me whole,
I will never cease to praise him,
I'll shout it while eternity rolls.

He touched me; oh, he touched me,
And oh the joy that floods my soul!

Something happened and now I know
He touched me and made me whole.

(© Bill and Gloria Gaither. Used with permission.)

The words took on new meaning for me that day.

When I finally opened my eyes and dried my tears, Mr. Everheart smiled at me. "How was it?"

I sat up straight, rubbed my eyes and tried to adjust to being back in the bright and cheery office.

"It was awesome! You wouldn't believe what I saw. Jesus let me sit on his lap while he healed my heart. The dark spots are gone!" I pressed a hand over my chest. "He healed all the wounds in my heart."

"I knew He could do it. That's why he came."

I scratched my head and thought for a moment. *Should I tell him about the rose? Oh, sure, why not?*

"I almost picked a yellow rose for you."

"That would have been special." He grinned. Then he gave me a hug and sent me off.

As I walked backed to the dorm, I took another look at my hands. *I'll be jiggered. They're still clean.*

I knocked on Mrs. Spencer's apartment door. When my dorm parent opened it, she looked surprised. "Lizzy, what happened to you? Your face is shining!"

She became the second of many to hear my story that day. We rejoiced together.

Before I went to sleep that night, I wrote a poem in my new book about my visit with Jesus:

His Hands

Dear Jesus, you know I love you,
I said to him one night,
As he put his arms around me
And held me very tight.

Getting Rid of the Dark Spots

Then as I sat upon his lap,
He showed his hands to me.
It was then I began to realize
What it cost to set me free.

I told him I was sorry
I had caused him so much pain.
And though my sins were many
His death removed the stain.

I thanked him for forgiveness
As I wept upon His chest.
Just knowing how much he loved me
Has put my heart at rest.

He washed away my dark spots,
And forgave my every sin.
He healed my deepest wounds.
And gave me peace within.

Lizzy Bauman, 1962

XXVII

Graduation

NEAR THE MIDDLE OF OUR SENIOR YEAR, THE SALESMAN FROM JOSTENS came to our school and presented a beautiful array of rings to our class. He said he would put "NC" in the center of each, for Nebraska Christian. We could put our birthstone on it. And, of course, we each put on our first and last initials.

Exciting day for everyone—except for me. I had no money to buy a ring. The cheap ones without a stone cost twenty-five to thirty-five dollars. The ones with gemstones were worth much more. I was already in danger of not graduating because I couldn't pay my school bill, so there was no way I could even remotely wish for one.

I helped Robin pick out a ring with a sapphire stone. I admired the beautiful blue gem. "It's too bad you can't get one," she said.

I shrugged. "It's no big deal. It's just a ring."

A few months later, the salesman returned with the finished products—bright, shiny rings with a beautiful array of stones and emblems. I watched my classmates take possession of their new treasures. They slipped them on their fingers and showed them to each other. They looked so thrilled and radiant.

Finally, the salesman started packing up. "Hey, I have one more ring here. Who didn't pick theirs up?"

"What are the initials on it?" someone asked.

"EB," he said.

"That's Elizabeth Bauman."

"But I didn't order one." I stood there bewildered. "I didn't have no money to buy it."

Our class president picked it up and handed it to me. "It's all yours, Lizzy. All of us got together, chipped in a buck or two, and bought one for you. You've been such an inspiration to us. We've watched how hard you've had to work to make it through these past three years. You deserve it."

I stood there with my hand over my mouth, my eyes wide like saucers.

"Well, go ahead and put it on," Robin said.

I slipped it on the fourth finger of my left hand. Tears trickled down my cheeks as I held it out and admired it. Then all my class-mates gathered around and hugged the life out of me.

~

Near the end of the school year, our class of sixteen students secretly planned a "sneak day"—with the help of Mr. Everheart, of course. We left at 5:00 in the morning, my younger roommate still fast asleep, and headed for Lincoln, the capital of Nebraska. Mr. Everheart and a couple of other chaperones drove us there.

We went to the Nebraska State Historical Society Museum and saw firsthand all the things I'd only read about in books. There were weapons used in the Old West and displays of how Native Americans and pioneers had lived.

As we looked at the primitive homes of the early settlers, I nudged my friend Robin on the arm. "Looks like my house."

"Mine, too." We chuckled.

We left the museum and stopped at the National Bank of Commerce. The banker took us into the inner vault and showed us the five hundred and the one thousand dollar bills.

"Whoa! I ain't never seen that much money in my whole life! I could use a couple of those to pay off my bill at school."

Robin elbowed me. "Couldn't we all?"

After leaving the bank, we toured the State Penitentiary. The wardens allowed us to walk past some of the prisoners and then took us to an empty cell and locked the door. I felt a little jolt when the heavy metal door clanged shut.

Okay, this is scary. At least I'm in here with my friends. I'll make sure I behave myself, so I'll never be locked up like this.

There were only a few of us, but they crammed us into a small space with metal cots on either side. Just as I began to feel dizzy from the close quarters, and the idea of being stuck inside forever, they opened the cell door. I hurried out of there and wended my way back through all the iron doors.

It feels so good to be outdoors again. I wonder how those people feel after being locked up for a long time?

For lunch, we had to walk a couple of blocks to a restaurant. At one street corner, we stopped for a red light.

When it turned green, I didn't move. Sandra, one of the smartest girls in our class, said, "Come on, it's green. Let's go."

I hesitated. "How do you know the cars are gonna stop, so I don't git run over?"

"Heavens to Betsy! Where did you grow up? Out in the sticks?" She grabbed my hand and dragged me across to the other side.

"Well, I ain't never crossed a street at a stoplight before. I don't know how it works. We only have six stop signs in my town."

We ate lunch at King's Restaurant, where they charged one price, regardless of how much we ate. The guys took advantage of that offer. Most of them had second helpings of King's burgers with double Angus Beef patties and fresh cut French fries. Could they ever eat a lot! Robin and I had grilled chicken with lettuce, tomatoes, onions and mayo. No fries, as we had enough zits as it was.

After lunch, we visited the Back to the Bible Broadcast, a well-known Christian radio station. We even met Theodore Epp, a preacher I had listened to many times on the radio.

When I saw the Capitol building, it took my breath away. I had never seen anything so ornate in my life.

We passed through the State Library. "Holy Smoke! Look at all those books," Robin said.

"Yeah, I ain't never seen that many in my whole life. I wonder if someone has read them all." I smiled to myself, remembering that I had exactly the same thought when I first saw the library at Nebraska Christian.

For the last event of the trip, and perhaps the most thrilling, we took a flight over Lincoln in an airplane. If going up a 12 foot ladder scared me, you can imagine what the thought of flying thousands of feet above the city did to me.

I grabbed Robin's arm. "I ain't goin' up that high."

"But you'll miss all the fun," Robin said. "Come on. You can go with me. I'll hang on to you."

I reluctantly climbed into the plane. When it took off, I pinched my eyes shut and wrapped my arms around myself.

Robin thumped me on my arm. "Open your eyes! Look out the window."

When I finally had the courage to peek, I couldn't believe what I saw. Everything looked so breathtaking from above. We could see the Capitol building and the rest of the city. Cars looked like toys and people like tiny specks.

This must be how God sees us, only he's even higher up. How small must I appear to him? And yet, he loves me. I'm utterly dumbfounded.

After landing safely, we stopped briefly at the Lincoln Air Force Base on our way out of town. We watched several planes take off and land. It boggled my mind how a machine that heavy could overcome gravity and fly up into the clouds. It made our recent flight seem even more astounding.

We arrived back at school only a half hour before our senior banquet. While we were gone, the juniors had decorated the dining hall with royal blue and white streamers. They emblazoned our theme, "Occupying Till He Comes," across the wall in giant letters, sprinkled with glitter. To enter the room, we walked through a pergola covered with flowers make from tissue paper. With the lights dimmed, it felt heavenly.

The evening was the equivalent of a prom in a secular high school, but there was no dancing here. My parents approved of that.

The guys who had eaten so much at noon appeared to be hungry again and devoured the turkey dinner with gusto. Some of us were so tuckered out, we had difficulty listening to the program. After a good night's rest, we tackled our final term papers and exams.

~

A few days later, Mr. Everheart asked my classmate Sandra and me to come to his office. Now what had we done to merit such an invitation?

"Good news, young ladies!" he said. "Miss Wilson and I calculated your grade point averages for the time you've been in this school. Sandra, after your two years here, you have a 3.82 average. You will be giving the Valedictory Address at the commencement service for your class."

"Bummer!" Sandra crossed her arms, narrowed her eyes and let out a sigh of exasperation. "I don't want to give a speech."

"It's an honor, Sandra," he said. Then he turned to me.

Since Sandra hadn't been thrilled with her news, I held my breath and waited for what he would say next. My palms grew clammy.

"Lizzy, after your three years, you have an average of 3.81. You will be giving the Salutatory Address at the Baccalaureate Service the Sunday evening before commencement."

I covered my mouth with my hand.

"Are you sure? I thought Jenny did better than I did."

"I'm very sure." He smiled.

My heart did some gymnastic tricks as I contemplated what this meant. I'd never had to do anything that terrifying before.

Git a grip, Lizzy.

"If either of you want some ideas or help with your speeches, let me know," Mr. Everheart said.

Sandra left the office in a hurry. I started to get up to follow her but Mr. Everheart lifted a hand. "Could you stay for a minute, Lizzy? I have something else to tell you."

I sank back in my chair, my heart pounding. What now? Was he going to take back the offer since I hadn't finished paying off my debt and couldn't graduate?

"I just found out last night that one of the board members has kindly offered to finish paying all you owe. Your debt is gone, Lizzy. You can graduate with the rest of your class."

Tears welled in my eyes. "Really? Hey, God does answer prayer!"

Mr. Everheart sat back in his chair beaming.

I ran back to the dorm and knocked on Mrs. Spencer's door. When she opened it, I blurted out my good news, unable to keep it inside a moment longer. "I placed second highest in my class, Mrs. Spencer!" The words tumbled out. "Mr. Everheart asked me to give a speech at graduation."

"Congratulations, Lizzy! I knew you could do it." She gave me a hug.

"And guess what else?"

"More good news?"

"Yes, one of the board members paid off my school account. I can graduate with the rest of my class."

"That's incredible news! I'm so happy for you. God has been so good to you."

"He sure has," I said. I raced off to tell Robin and my other friends.

≈

Mr. Everheart helped me write my speech. At the Baccalaureate service, I marched bravely to the podium and tried not to stammer as I spoke to an audience of hundreds of people. My knocking knees sounded like a woodpecker on the roof to me, but no one else seemed to notice.

"Fellow graduates, teachers, parents and friends. Three years ago, when Mr. Spencer spoke at our church and told about this school opening, I couldn't believe it. My acceptance letter from Mr. Everheart was nothing short of a miracle. My life has been drastically changed by what I have learned here. I want to share a poem with you that I wrote about God's grace to me."

Blemished Heart

I'm a picture of God's grace
Hanging here for all to see;
I'm the masterpiece of my Creator,
He painted me perfectly.

He chose just the right colors,
Then joyfully painted his best,
To create a unique picture
That was different from the rest.

He was pleased with his handiwork
And hung it up in a special place.
But the picture got neglected
And looked an awful disgrace.

Careless people marred the image
And splattered it with fears.
When the Master saw what happened
He picked it up with tears.

He carefully restored the picture,
And loved it all the more;
Then added a few new touches
To make it better than before.

I'm a picture of God's grace
Hanging here for all to see;
Some day I'll hang in his gallery
For all eternity!

I took a deep breath. "God has certainly added a lot of 'new touches' to my life here at Nebraska Christian." I ended my speech with the words of Helen Keller, "I am only one, but still, I am one. I can't do everything, but still I can do something. And because I cannot do everything, I will not refuse to do the something that I can do."

In that moment I determined in my heart to do whatever I could to make the world a better place to live.

The couple that paid off my school debt came to my graduation. Mr. Everheart introduced them to me.

"Thank you so much for what you did for me," I said. I gave them both a hug.

"Mr. Everheart told us how hard you worked to finish high school. You made us all proud."

≈

Upon graduating, I had to part ways with my dear classmates and teachers. I didn't want to leave them. They meant so much to me. I vowed to keep in touch with them.

My sadness turned to apprehension, as I would have to return to my home for three months, until my classes started at Grace Bible Institute in Omaha in the fall. Jimmy had left for the U.S. navy in November of 1961, a year and a half before I graduated. I would miss him. Clyde joined the navy a few months later, so I wouldn't have to deal with him. All I'd have to be concerned about was working and making enough money to go back to school—and staying out of trouble with Dad.

Maybe I can do it with your help, God.

I recalled one of my favorite Bible verses: "I can do all things through him who gives me strength." Philippians 4:13 Onward!

XXVIII

Last Summer
Before College

IN ORDER TO STAY AWAY FROM HOME, I WORKED LONG HOURS THAT summer after graduation. I not only cleaned the motel and helped Mrs. Jansen vacuum the church, but I also helped ladies from our church clean out their attics, do housework, iron or whatever else they asked me to do.

I saved all my money to go to Bible College, which cost fifteen hundred dollars a year instead of five hundred dollars, like I had paid for my tuition, room and board at Nebraska Christian. It helped that I received over two hundred dollars from friends and relatives for my graduation. I socked all my money away in the bank until classes started in September of 1962.

In our final year at Nebraska Christian, most of the sixteen students in my class chose to continue their education. Several of the girls went into nurses training. One fellow joined the army, and quite a few of us enrolled at Grace Bible Institute in Omaha, Nebraska.

None of my family had ever gone beyond high school, but I wanted a better education so I could use it to help other people. I even dreamed of being a missionary after reading *Shadow of the Almighty* and *Through Gates of Splendor* by Elizabeth Elliot. Reading about the lives of Jim Elliot and his fellow missionaries had a profound effect on me. Since I had promised God that I would serve him the rest of my life for rescuing me from my home, preparing for such service at a Bible College became a natural choice.

"Why do you want to go to school?" Dad asked. "You'll only git married and have kids. All that money will be wasted. I'll bet you'll be married before you turn twenty-one."

"No, I won't," I said.

He made me write that promise in his Bible and sign it. I did— and I kept it.

Anyway, I wasn't so sure I wanted to marry and have children, not if it was like what I had experienced growing up. I loved kids, though, and wanted to be an elementary teacher. After Bible College, I planned to enroll in teacher's college at the University of Nebraska in Lincoln for the 1965-66 school year. My goal was to eventually go to Ecuador to teach missionary children in Quito.

≈

In the meantime, I set some smaller goals for that summer. First, I set out to obtain my driver's license. I turned eighteen that August. Most of my friends had been driving since they were sixteen.

We had a 1952 Studebaker in 1962—well used by the time my parents bought it. The car's gray-green paint had long since faded or chipped off. Few parts still worked. We could see the road through the floorboard. Of course, it didn't have power steering, so one of the boys screwed a "steering knob" to the wheel to make it easier to turn corners. It had a manual stick shift and a barely-working clutch. We stepped on the gas pedal, which we called the "foot-feed," to make it go. I had a hard time coordinating my hands and feet at first, and the car stalled often.

Mom never drove over 35-40 miles per hour, so I scared her spitless when I first sat in the driver's seat.

"Slow down. We ain't goin' to no fire." She gripped the door handle.

"I ain't even drivin' the speed limit."

"That don't matter none. Slow down, or I ain't practicin' with you no more."

I read the manual and practiced driving with my mom a few times. How hard could it be? When I was ready, we drove to Central City to the license office where I passed the written test with flying colors. Then the examiner took me out to the parking lot, while Mom stayed in the office. When I started the car, it came to life with a loud roar. "Turn that off and come back when you have the muffler fixed," he said.

After he went back into the building, I dragged my mom outside and hollered at her, "Why do we have to drive an old jalopy like this? Now I can't git my license."

"We'll git a new muffler as soon as we can afford one," she said.

"Oh, sure, I'll be fifty years old before that happens."

Some time later, my dad installed a new muffler, and I applied again. Thank goodness, the examiner didn't complain about any of the other deficiencies of the car, and I passed.

My mom let me drive the eleven miles home. Out in the country, I slowed for a corner. I rolled down the window to make a right hand signal, holding my arm straight up. As I started to make the turn, the driver's door flew open. I tried to hang on to it and close it again, but the car ended up in the ditch with me nearly falling out on the road in the process. Fortunately, it was a shallow ditch, and I was able to back out on my own. I was a bit tense on the way home.

"This stupid car ain't worth a hill o' beans. We could git killed in this thing."

"It's all we can afford, so stop complainin'."

≈

The summer after I graduated would be the last I ever spent in my home. Soon after that, my dad found a job driving a road grader for the county. He had dreamed of doing that for many years, and it would be a lot easier than farm work.

My family moved into a house in the town of Clarks. For the first time, they had an indoor bathroom, and I wouldn't even be there to enjoy that luxury.

In September of 1962, I moved my belongings to Grace Bible Institute in Omaha. My whole future lay ahead of me. With God's help, I had been able to survive and then extricate myself from my abusive home. With eternal gratitude for what he had done for me, I would serve him with all my heart, wherever he wanted me. I didn't know exactly what my future held, but I knew who held it, and I felt safe in that knowledge.

Epilogue

WHEN JIMMY RETURNED FROM THREE YEARS IN THE NAVY, HE MARRIED Kay, a friend of Lizzy's from Nebraska Christian. Lizzy had introduced them before he left. He eventually became a long-distance trucker and hauled merchandise all over America. To their great disappointment, he and Kay could never have any children.

Clyde also spent three years in the Navy. Years later, he moved to Columbus and worked in a factory. He didn't marry until he was in his early forties. He and his wife had no children.

Molly finished high school and later worked as a dishwasher in a hotel. In her early thirties, she married a trucker friend of Jimmy's. They had no children. She died at the age of forty-eight of ovarian cancer.

Sherry married several times and had four children. She eventually became disabled as the result of an industrial accident and couldn't work the rest of her life.

Dad worked until he became ill with Parkinson's disease. He spent the last twelve years of his life wasting away in a nursing home. He died at 83 years of age.

Mom went to live with Clyde and his wife in her later years. She died at the age of 89.

Lizzy worked her way through three years of Bible College, earning money cleaning a house every afternoon for various women, including a Jewish rabbi's wife. Later, she worked at an auto parts store in downtown Omaha. On the side, she gave haircuts to some of the male students for half the price the barber charged. She stayed in the city during the summer, boarding with a couple from her church, and seldom went home to Clarks.

Lizzy enjoyed school, had a variety of interesting roommates, and played trombone in the band and a brass trio. She occasionally dated, but the only one she seriously considered as husband material ended the friendship when he saw how determined she was to go into missionary work. He felt he wasn't cut out for that, and he wanted to take over his dad's farm.

She liked one other fellow, Pierre Boulon, but he was from Canada, and would soon be on his way back there. However, he stayed in Omaha after graduation to finish building a house for one of his professors—and came for a haircut in late June. As Lizzy cut his hair, Pierre joked with her. "If you don't do a good job, I won't marry you."

She chuckled. "Maybe I'll put a few nicks in it then."

Before graduating from Grace in June of 1965, Lizzy applied to the University of Nebraska teacher's college in Lincoln to learn to be an elementary school teacher. She was getting closer to her goal of going to the mission field.

On August 13, 1965, a month before teacher's college started, Pierre, whom she had been friends with for the past three years at Grace, but had only dated for seven weeks, asked her to marry him.

Lizzy was shocked. "I'm s'posed to go to teacher's college next month."

Pierre pulled an engagement ring out of his pocket.

She gasped. "You're serious, aren't you?"

"Yes, I love you and want you to be my wife."

She let him slip the ring on to her left hand and then they kissed for the first time.

Lizzy withdrew her registration at the University of Nebraska and married Pierre in December of 1965. She was twenty-one years and four months old. She had kept the promise that she had written in the family Bible.

Seven weeks after they married, Lizzy and Pierre went for mission orientation classes in Missouri, then studied Spanish at Rio Grande Bible Institute in Edinburg, Texas for a year. In February of

1968, with their three-month-old son John, they boarded a plane for Central America. Lizzy and Pierre taught at a Bible school and pastored a small country church. They returned to North America in May of 1969, and settled down in Canada near Pierre's family. They added three more sons to their happy family—Peter, James and Andrew. Lizzy became a Canadian citizen in 1971.

Lizzy always felt badly about not finishing her schooling, so in 1990, she enrolled as a part-time student at Tyndale Seminary in Toronto. She graduated in 1997 with a Master of Divinity degree, majoring in counseling. She started her own counseling practice and helped many, many people find out how to get rid of the blemishes in their own hearts.

Endnotes

1 Bohlken Ph.D, Bob. *Listening to Rural Midwestern Idioms/Folk Sayings*. (Maryville, MO. Snaptail Press, Division of Images Unlimited, 2007), Page 2.

2 Ibid., Page 21.

3 Ibid., Page 8.

4 Ibid., Page 19.

A portion of the royalties from book sales will be donated to Freedom Readers, an organization Fern has been involved in since 2010. Freedom Readers seeks to improve reading skills in low wealth communities by providing one-to-one literacy tutoring and free books for home libraries.

www.freedomreaders.org